# Usher Me Home

# Usher Me Home

STEVE HAMBY

Copyright © 2010 by Steve Hamby.

Library of Congress Control Number: 2010909547
ISBN: Hardcover 978-1-4535-2923-2
Softcover 978-1-4535-2922-5
Ebook 978-1-4535-2924-9

All rights reserved. No part of this book may be reproduced or transmitted in any form or by any means, electronic or mechanical, including photocopying, recording, or by any information storage and retrieval system, without permission in writing from the copyright owner.

This is a work of fiction. Names, characters, places and incidents either are the product of the author's imagination or are used fictitiously, and any resemblance to any actual persons, living or dead, events, or locales is entirely coincidental.

This book was printed in the United States of America.

To order additional copies of this book, contact:
Xlibris Corporation
1-888-795-4274
www.Xlibris.com
Orders@Xlibris.com

This, my first published work, is dedicated to my children, Stephanie and Jared, whose love and courageous spirit inspire me on a daily basis: And my wife, Phyllis, whose support and love encourages me to accomplish more than I could ever imagine.

# CHAPTER 1

GREG BAGWELL WASN'T prepared for the bad news he was handed six months ago, but over these past months, he realized there wasn't much he could do about the inoperable brain tumor, so he was preparing himself for the inevitable. His oncologist, Rob Slaughter, was candid with Greg when the diagnosis was confirmed, letting him know that in all likelihood, he wouldn't last more than a year. Rather than crawling up in a corner and quietly disappearing from the scene of life, he had determined that he would make the most of the hand he'd been dealt. With every ounce of his being, he intended to make as much impact for the kingdom as humanly possible in his remaining days.

I had no idea of the impact that he would make on those around him during his last days, nor was I prepared for the magnitude of the transformation that I would experience. That would be made painfully and wonderfully aware to me within the next few days. Greg was not just an inspirational and determined individual that was in his final days, but he was also my dad. We hadn't always been close either, mostly due to the impact on me and others in his life because of his other disease, which nearly took him from us just a few years ago – his alcoholism. During the twenty years of substance abuse, Dad was a virtual stranger in his own home. He had, however, become a changed man over the past few years, since he'd worked so diligently to suppress the demon of alcoholism. There was a time when no one who knew him well thought he would or could change, but he proved us all wrong.

Dad had left a coveted corporate job in downtown Chicago just a couple of years ago, in November 2008. He had put over twenty-five years of his life into his career as a sales leadership executive in the financial services industry. He worked his way up the corporate ladder from his entry-level sales position, holding about as many positions as he had years with the company. Dad's line had been that he was married to his job one year longer than to my mother, Sherri. In the end, it was the company that chose for Greg to leave instead of him being the driver of the decision that fateful November two years ago. He'd become just another statistic in the litany of corporate downsizings.

I'd been amazed at his resolve and his strength during what seemed to me to be a real slap in his face as reward for all the dedicated years of service. As with so many companies as of late, it appeared that his company was just putting more money in someone's coffer at the top of the organization; it wasn't like they weren't profitable and needed to cut jobs to stay afloat during the tough economic times that faced the country in 2008. Some companies had to make cuts to survive, but not Greg's. The company Gregory Bagwell worked for was like so many others; they disguised job eliminations under a veil of "need to survive." They targeted those long-tenured employees in middle to upper management, who were highly compensated, and simply cut those jobs to bring more profits to the bottom line.

Once the announcement had been made that his job had been eliminated, Dad (in what became usual fashion for him) simply stated that God was sovereign. He trusted Him fully, and He was apparently ready for a change for Dad. At peace seemed to understate Dad's state of mind during this time. In many ways, he seemed to become stronger and more resolute after this downsizing of his career and loss of his livelihood. Dad was continually giving thanks to God for His strength and power, but I had a really hard time believing that anyone could really put their trust in anything other than themselves these days. What happened to Dad seemed cruel and unfair, at least to me.

Life in general just didn't seem fair, and I was convinced that God (who I believed in) was not a very loving higher power. Based on all I'd seen in my twenty-two years, it had become increasingly apparent to me that God didn't care about us as individuals. After all, I'd graduated from the ultraconservative Christian college of Liberty University in Lynchburg, Virginia, with my business major nearly six months ago, and He hadn't answered my prayers and need for a job. That was just the beginning of my long list of disappointments and signs that God seemed to have written me off His list.

When I should have been starting my own career or at least gaining some practical experience, I was working at the local Hampshire Landscaping Company, located in the small town of Hampshire, Illinois, about fifty miles west of downtown Chicago, until I could find a real job. Not that I didn't like the outdoors as I loved being in nature, but more for hiking and camping rather than sculpting landscapes for people who were in those jobs and careers that I coveted. The work was fairly relaxing, though, and something I'd become familiar with over the warm summers in the northwestern burbs, working summer jobs with another privately owned landscaping company located in the neighboring town of Elgin, Illinois.

This time, though, the job was a little more personal, and I had a greater sense of satisfaction since I was helping Dad at this landscaping business he'd started from scratch a year ago. He needed the help in his growing business, and I needed gainful employment. Besides, I was the most trustworthy employee he could have on the payroll, truly watching out for his best interest. The God thing seemed to be working for Dad these days in dealing with his death sentence with the brain tumor, so who was I to question the way he approached life. He was a content man in spite of this new trial that life had dealt to him. I don't recall the exact chapter and verse but know one of Dad's favorite scriptures from the Bible was something about being content in all circumstances. As I recall, this scripture even suggested that one should "count it all joy." I'm not sure how that applied to my everyday life, though, and firmly believed that God understood that I had reason to not be content given my own lot in life. Dad taught me over the years that contentment, regardless of circumstance, was joy. He differentiated this to happiness, which was contentment due to favorable circumstances. Dad strove for a joyful life, and seeing his positive mental attitude, regardless of circumstance, his joy was something I desperately wanted for my life as well.

Dad even decided that it was time to start a new hobby two years ago after his "corporate retirement" at forty-eight. He didn't actually retire, but that seemed to be the word used when one was over a certain age and their job was eliminated. This was yet another of many corporate lies that didn't seem to endear people to their jobs these days. The days of companies being as loyal to the employees as they expected employees to be to them seemed a thing of the past, something of my grandparent's generation.

So what hobby did Dad take up at forty-eight? Of all the things he could have done, he decided to start oil painting. As far back as I could recall, he had a very rudimentary talent for doodling, but nothing I'd ever seen that indicated he might have some hidden talent to paint. Mom actually encouraged him after he made it known that he'd like to try his hand at oil painting by visiting a local art supply store in nearby Algonquin (a community, exploding with growth, in Northwest Illinois). She made her contribution to his hobby by buying an easel, a variety of canvases, every size and shape of brush, palate knives, and enough tubes of paint that we could have easily used them to paint the outside of the house.

The first couple of paintings Dad completed were beyond amateurish, looking more like finger paintings elementary school kids would do as their first experimentation with paint. They were in a word – pitiful. He seemed interested in landscapes, but I believed that he should have explored a different hobby, based on the unnatural talent all of us saw on those first attempts. Minimally, we thought he should invest in a class or two or three. In his first attempt at any sort of artwork in his life two years ago, he chose to paint a simple landscape.

Dad's first painting contained trees that were out of proportion, limbs seeming to stop in the middle of nowhere. The sparse limbs of the tree appeared almost as thick as the trunk of the tree. The leaves and the fruit he added to the tree didn't just miss the mark; they didn't even get in the vicinity of the mark. Blobs of paint appeared to be slapped on to represent fruit, many not even connecting to the tree, just seeming to float in midair. He even had bold yellow and white stripes coming from the top corner across the canvass, apparently representing sunlight – . At least that's what I think he was attempting in this piece of "art." The rays of light actually resembled an abstract yellow and white rainbow that had lost its curve, broad at the base and thin at the top. When asked why he decided to paint abstracts, he looked at us like we had three heads. "That's not abstract," he would insist. Could have fooled all of us.

We were all hopeful that Mom had kept the receipts for all the paint supplies, so she could get at least a refund on some portion of the hobby expenditure. But Dad just kept trying different techniques, and once his borderline obsessive-compulsive disorder (OCD) kicked in, his perfectionism transferred onto the canvas, and his art started to resemble, well . . . art.

Within a couple of months from his first attempt at a painting, the meticulous attention to detail, hues of color and texture he had experimented with, came to life on the canvas, making his creations look like something that might hang proudly in someone's home or office. We tried to encourage him to sell some of his paintings, but he was either overly humble and modest or he was fishing for more compliments when he declined our suggestion. I felt like it was the former, but if his ego was anything like mine, it was probably a bit of the latter, too. He loved to give many of his paintings as gifts to family and friends, and we were all extremely grateful that he waited before he started to do that. Otherwise, he might have truly disappointed to find a few of his gifts in garages or worse.

He spent untold hours, painting a wide variety of landscapes. If he incorporated people into a painting, he would add them with a view from their back side or, at most, a side view incorporated into the canvas scene, which became one of his painting signatures. Light appeared in various forms in most of his creations as well, becoming another expected element of his work.

One particular painting that he completed in those first few months of his new hobby really "cranked my tractor," as my great-uncle Paul (a deep-rooted Southerner) used to say when he was really impressed with something. It made me realize that Dad might actually have a talent for painting. It was a depiction of our family on a traditional outing from twenty years ago. In the painting of our family of four, he had included me as a toddler, sitting atop my dad's shoulders with our hands intertwined, keeping me balanced on his broad shoulders. Mom was pictured holding my older sister Lindsey's still small hand in a crowd of people, who all appeared to be enjoying a fireworks display. Based on the expressions captured on the faces, everyone was having a great time at the Independence Day festivities.

In the painting, our family (which stood out in more color than the rest of the onlookers) was looking skyward and pointing at fireworks that were bursting in vibrant colors in the distance, lighting up a clear night sky over a lake. As usual with Dad's paintings, it was taken from behind its subjects, with only backs of heads or side profiles visible. The sky was filled with a brilliant rainbow of color and lights, depicting the fireworks display, penetrating the overall darkness of the painting set at night. The reflections and the lighting on the faces made me feel like I was right back at the scene in the small town of Fontana on Lake Geneva, Wisconsin. This is where we spent most Fourth of July celebrations since we'd moved into the northwestern suburbs of Chicago, about forty miles due south of the Wisconsin border town of Lake Geneva. This, like many things in our lives, had become a holiday tradition for our immediate family. The painting was breathtaking and brought back wonderful memories of our family during a much simpler time of life. Fortunately, we were able to enjoy the *Bagwell Fourth* painting often as it hung in the sunroom of the family home.

Though Dad continued to enjoy this newfound hobby, he decided a year ago to go back to work. This time around, he wanted more independence rather than the interdependence of a corporate career. Something he could put his own stamp on, where he could call his own shots. He loved the outdoors and spent untold hours manicuring his own lawn, berms, and flower beds. We all thought it was a good fit when he decided to start up a landscape business. He liked being around people and especially enjoyed using his creative flair, whether on canvas or outside, creating awesome landscapes that could be enjoyed both inside and outside.

Since our small town and neighboring towns were the next natural expansion west of Chicago's O'Hare airport, housing had been booming even in a depressed housing market that had become the norm in most areas of the country in 2008. The mortgage debacle that plagued most residential housing starts hadn't seemed to be as prevalent in this area, based on the growth explosion. Cornfields in these wide-open expanses seemed to be growing new three – to four-bedroom homes with two – and three-car garages while corn still grew in and around the new crop of homes. Dad's landscape business became known quickly in the area, and word of mouth became his primary source of advertising. Reputation, he soon discovered, combined with value and quality of work became the keys to success in this line of work.

Little did I know that there was actually a fair amount of business acumen needed to run a small owner-operated business. Maybe this actually could be a place where I'd have an opportunity to begin to use my newly earned business degree. That is, if I choose to take over the family business after Dad's passing. Dad would say, "Maybe the reason you can't find a corporate job right now is that God's guiding you into this business to take it over permanently, Jared." To which I would reply, "Dad, do you really think God cares what line of work I go into or who I work for? I don't even think *your* pastor Bob would buy into that one. Come on, be real."

# CHAPTER 2

WHY IN THE world Dad decided to not just prepare his own funeral but pick the date and get it on all his friends and relatives' calendars made absolutely no sense to me, but those that knew him well realized this wasn't that out of character for him. A couple of family friends even asked me if I thought he was planning his own demise a couple of days before the upcoming funeral. Why else would you plan your own funeral, right?

That was absolutely not in the cards. Dad was not only too chicken to do himself in, but he had told me six months previously when he found out about his untreatable brain tumor that he feared his reward in heaven could be impacted if he took his own life, whatever that meant. I just didn't question it but rather took it as a comfort that no matter how painful the remainder of his short life would get, he wouldn't exit any sooner than the "Big Guy upstairs" decided was his designated time.

"Dad, now tell me again why in the world you want to have this funeral before you actually . . ." – I paused because I couldn't say the "d" word as it had such a finality to it – "You know . . . pass on?"

"You can say 'die,' son, 'go see Jesus face-to-face,' 'kick the bucket,' 'croak,' 'die.'" Dad had such a nonchalant attitude toward death, which seemed weird to me, but certainly didn't to him. He was as comfortable talking about death as he was talking about life.

"I'm more comfortable with passing on, which is what Mom's family always said, Dad, and besides . . . ," I continued, trying to be sensitive to the subject of this crazy idea of a funeral while he sat there listening, "doesn't this in the least bit seem a little morbid?"

"Jared," he interrupted with a slight cock of his head and squint of his eyes, looking at me like I was the one with three heads. "I think this is one of the most amazing ideas I've ever had, God inspired, of course. I'm looking forward to this more than you can possibly imagine."

He had that right, at least the part about his looking forward to it! I raised my eyebrows, took a deep breath, and just sighed, realizing I didn't need to understand. One thing that made absolutely no sense to me was how would anyone know what was inspired by God Almighty, anyway? It's not like He could talk to us, right? I'd heard people say things like this in the past and wondered why others seemed to have some kind of communication with God when all I saw was a one-way line of communication to Him, certainly nothing from Him.

"All right, all right . . . I know you need my help with the remaining details and the arrangements, so I'm here for you, but I have to admit, Dad, this is really bizarre for me." I rolled my eyes, scrunching my face up in disgust, as I flipped my hands upward with palms up. "A movie theater as the venue, for Christ's sake . . ."

Immediately, I was chided. "Jared, please don't use Christ's name in vain. You know that's one thing I can't tolerate."

"I'm sorry, Dad. I always forget you even consider *that* as using His name in vain." I paused and blew out air as if that would remove some of my stress about the subject, pausing again slightly before I continued, "You know . . . Mom just cracked up when she heard what you were planning and told me, 'It's your father, Bud, just go with it. You know you'll not change his stubborn mind when he makes it up, and he is absolutely convinced this is what he's being led to do. And what more appropriate place than a movie theater, given his love of movies'!"

At that, this fifty-year-old man, who really didn't even look sick but certainly looked every day of his fifty years, just smiled that broad, tight-lipped crooked smile, raising his left eyebrow only, slightly looking downward, indicating that he'd won this round and was ready to move on.

Shifting gears out of what he knew was an uncomfortable discussion for me, Dad matter-of-factly said, "Let's go eat."

"You got it, Dad. All this talk has me starved, given the topic of discussion. Whatcha think 'bout a rack o' ribs?" I had been around enough Southerners in my twenty-two years that it came pretty natural for me to shift my dialect into a Southern accent in exaggerated form when it served my purpose. Anyone who knew me well knew that my use of a Southern accent happened when I was either tired, just messing around, or nervous about the topic at hand, pretty obvious that it was the latter this time.

"Sounds lik'a plan." Dad threw back as drawn-out as he could deliver, knowing he was mocking my lazy-sounding speech. We both realized that we could turn it on like a light switch when we felt the need or just playing around. It was at its best when we would mock one of his favorite cousins, Renee, who was already on her way up to Chicagoland for the funeral from Jackson, Mississippi. She was a "hoot," as my dad would say, and this was an understatement. The woman could do stand-up comedy, just reading a restaurant menu or a church bulletin. "Let's head out, Bud."

Off we headed to Famous Dave's for some good ole ribs, not as good as what we used to get in Memphis at the Rendezvous or Gridley's, but not bad for a city north of the Mason-Dixon Line.

Lindsey was finally showing and definitely unable to hide it any longer. Her hubby of three years, John, was more than supportive and hadn't stopped smiling since they found out about the baby five and half months ago. Most would say he spoiled her rotten too, but that was OK by me, especially given what all of us had been through over the past several years. By the world's standards, most would say that my sibling and I had been spoiled, but the world's standards typically only involved material things.

It was killing Lindsey, my twenty-five-year-old sibling, to think she'd be bringing their baby into this world without Dad in the picture, but the memories this child would eventually hear about Grandpa Greg would surely make the kid feel like he or she had known Grandpa its entire life. Dad had already earned the nickname of 'Grandpa' when he was younger than me and in college. His profile (especially when he had hair) did resemble that of the character from an old black-and-white sitcom I'd seen once or twice in old reruns. I think it was called the *Munsters* – some early sitcom from a bygone era in which slapstick comedy was evidently funny. In the handful of episodes I saw, I just didn't get it. Oh well, it was a simpler time back then, and entertainment was . . . well, different.

With a tear forming in the corner of Lindsey's eye as she was allowing the heaviness of the inevitable loss of her father to weigh on her, John (in his thoughtful, discerning manner) simply wrapped his beefy arms around her waist from behind her small frame and snuggled his head in close to hers, without saying anything for a moment.

"So watcha thinkin'?" John asked, knowing his attempt at a Southern accent for a Chicago boy would give an instant smile to his bride, as he affectionately referred to Lindsey. Southern accents faked by native Chicagoans was just too funny. Add it to the short stature of the pocket Hercules, as we affectionately called workout-crazed John, and it was even more hilarious. He and Lindsey couldn't have been over four inches different in height and with Lindsey at a mere five feet three; John couldn't stretch to more than five feet seven. With both their blonde hair and steely blue eyes, they looked more like brother and sister than husband and wife. With my six-foot linebacker build, dark hair and complexion, Lindsey and I looked less like brother and sister than did she and her husband.

Letting out a slow breath and pursing her beautiful full lips, she barely got out an audible "Dad" in response to John's question, which caused the tear that was hanging in the corner of her eye to stream down her cheek, as a painful grimace painted across her pale china doll – like face.

John gently took the back of his hand and swiped the tear off her cheek, and as they both aimlessly stared upward at nothing in particular, he said, "I know . . . I still can't believe it. I know he won't be with us long, but I just so wish . . ."

"Don't say it 'cause I just won't allow myself to believe that God would take him from us before he has a chance to see . . ." Unable to complete her sentence, she slowly cupped her hands below the round ball in front of her that contained her child, too choked up to continue. John knew where she was going with this line of thinking, though, and it scared him to watch her strong faith and trust in God waning, even if for just a moment.

"Lindsey, nothing happens without it first going through God's hand. God didn't make your dad sick, but He certainly allowed it. Our – "

"I know," she interrupted. At this, she was getting slightly irritated at the spiritual lesson she didn't want to hear at the moment. "I know truth, John . . . Our finite minds cannot understand His ways, and we just have to trust Him, knowing his plan is perfect!" Realizing he'd said too much already, she added, "I'm just so angry at Him right now, and I know you'll say . . . He can take it. He's a big God, and He knows already what we're thinking. I'm so mad at Him right now, I could" – still trying to figure out her thoughts – "I could just crawl up and die myself."

John knew he just needed to cool it, and so he decided to just try to comfort her, changing the focus of discussion, hoping and praying that God would give him the words to say to help bring her back to her usual spiritual fitness. It pained him to see how her lack of trust was moving her away from the God of her childhood, the God of the universe, the God who he knew would be there to provide her the strength and power when she'd need it most. He hoped with all his might that this was just a temporary doubtful moment for Lindsey. Relying on herself would be the hard way, and he didn't want her to be so alone in dealing with what they all knew was coming – Dad's death. John only had one thought at this point in time – *God, please give me the words to help encourage her . . . I'm really struggling here and need you to speak through me to Lindsey.*

"Tell you what, Lindsey . . ." He changed the tone and direction of the conversation. "I'm starved and . . ." – while pointing at her round tummy – "I'm sure that little guy is too." Since they'd found out they were pregnant, John only referred to the baby as a he, which they didn't know and didn't want to know the sex of until they first lay eyes on the bundle of joy in the delivery room. "How about some barbeque or ribs? Famous Dave's is calling my name. Uh, oh, I hear Junior's name being called too." Faintly and in a babyish voice, he squirmed with his arms together while his entire being was pointing at Lindsey's stomach, "Junior, Junior, I know you're starvin', Marvin'. Would your mommy let you come and eat with me?"

Lindsey never tired of his antics and his attention to their baby girl, even if he insisted on calling her a him. At that, she just rolled her eyes, pulled her mouth sideways, and gave in while shaking her head in a no manner and did her best high-pitched baby voice in response, allowing her lips only slight movement as if she were a master ventriloquist. "OK, Daddy, I am sooo hungry, and for a girl, I bet I can eat you under the table . . . Hope they have a pink lemonade for me too. I looooove pink, don't you, Dadeo?" Whatever they were going to have, one thing was certain; with both parents' coloring and soft features, the baby would most likely look Scandinavian, which was not part of our ancestry, but certainly a dominant part of Mr. Nelson's heritage.

John already had light jackets in hand that he'd pulled out from the hall closet this mild fall day and was escorting Lindsey to the front door of their small two-bedroom bungalow. They adored the quaintness of their humble abode, which Dad had helped them fund a few months ago. Grandpa had told them that he was spending his inheritance with his loved ones before he was gone, so he could enjoy it with them. Getting to watch his kids enjoy it before he left was one more way he showed his "style" and his innate ability to still spoil his adult children.

Dad was one of those guys that just couldn't help himself when it came to giving. One of his gifts was giving, but since he was typically an anonymous giver, most would never know the depth of his charitable spirit. He would always insist that the right hand shouldn't know what the left hand was giving. This rule didn't apply to his family. It wasn't always material things or money, either he would clean up after we'd leave messes, picking up our rooms and bathrooms when Mom wasn't looking. Mom would reprimand him when he did this because she believed it didn't teach us to clean up after ourselves. Lindsey and I knew the real reason he did that was because he was a perfectionist, always wanting everything in its proper place. The whole family would kid around that Dad would be the guy in the nursing home someday that would spend his waking hours cleaning and straightening up the place. We would halfway kid that there'd be a list of nursing homes wanting him take up residency, knowing they'd have the cleanest, most orderly home that would attract new tenants and probably save a few bucks for staff to boot. Shoot, we thought they'd even subsidize him to live in their community.

I remember vividly when Lindsey went to college her freshman year at Judson College in nearby Elgin. She lived on campus, which was about thirty minutes from our parent's home, and a few weeks after getting her settled in, Mom and Dad dropped by to see how she was adjusting. Lindsey's dorm room looked like something out of *Homes and Gardens* for college living. It was picture perfect and not only organized but clean enough to eat off the floor. Dad was amazed at how immaculate Lindsey's room was and said to her that he thought it was hilarious that her assigned roommate was a neat freak, like him.

Lindsey just laughed and told Dad that it wasn't the roommate but rather Lindsey that was the neat freak. Dad, looking perplexed, said. "Wait a minute, your room was always a mess at home, and I can't count the number of times I picked up or cleaned your bathroom... What gives?" She just sheepishly looked at him and said, "Daddy, Jared and I always knew you'd eventually pick up and clean up after us, so – " Dad interrupted, "I did spoil you, didn't I?" Well, that was an understatement, which Lindsey absolutely couldn't deny. It was true, and quite frankly, we probably both took advantage of his perfectionism and OCD. Dad always said he was borderline OCD, but trust me, there was no borderline to it. The man was full-blown obsessive-compulsive. And absolutely no one could meet his standard. Although he could be irritating with his orderliness and cleanliness demands on others, we benefited from his obsessive orderliness more than enough to offset any minor irritation.

When the family discovered the television show *Monk*, which was about an obsessive-compulsive detective, we turned Dad onto the show. We loved watching the show with him and would crack up at scenes that we could have scripted by watching Dad. When we'd crack up, he routinely would throw the palms of his hands up and, with a questioning expression on his face, say, "What?" To which we would increase our laughter, and he'd just roll his eyes with an expression of whatever. We thought watching the show with him was much more humorous than the show itself, and it became one of the few television shows we'd try to make sure we watched as a family.

# CHAPTER 3

GREG BAGWELL WAS a sinner saved by grace, a man who'd become more humble in recent years, more of a spiritual leader in the family, and a man of God. For a man who'd become addicted to alcohol and prescription and nonprescription drugs and who could only think of himself for years, it was quite the transformation to see where he was today. Amazingly, his career continued to accelerate during the dark years, helping to self-confirm that he was functional and didn't really have a major issue with the substances. He had convinced himself, like so many addicts, that he could control it. After all, he could go days without mind-altering substances, but when he started, it was off to the races. He couldn't stop. Beginning to think he might have an issue after a number of years, it wasn't until months of blackouts, which were becoming the norm, that he finally conceded that he indeed had a problem. That revelation happened twelve long years ago.

The final straw that brought everything to a head was a family vacation of a lifetime – a trip to Maui and Oahu in July 1998. Mom and Dad wanted us to experience the paradise they had gone to for their honeymoon in 1983. Dad, unbeknownst to us, had started drinking before we left for O'Hare for the morning flight and continued throughout most of the eight-day vacation.

The day before the trip, he ventured to the backyard after seeing Lindsey and I enjoying the trampoline. In a playful mode, he charged toward the trampoline and leapt onto it, almost bouncing us off and while telling us to make room for him, laughing the whole time. It seemed to be just a playful time with Dad, but with his fears and inhibitions gone, he started doing carefree flips on the tramp. Next thing we knew, he did a backflip and landed right on his face. The bridge of his roman-shaped nose was busted and bleeding, and we had to tell him it was bleeding. He hadn't a clue. After another flip or two, he decided to go in the house to patch up the busted nose. "What was I thinking," he said more as a statement than a question, and we both wondered the same thing.

I now understand why they call alcoholism cunning, baffling, and powerful. It had a grip on Dad that was much stronger than his will. Looking back, we know he had lost all control over substance. Because Dad was a master at hiding his addiction, we really had no idea what we were dealing with. We just knew his behavior had become more erratic and unpredictable as time progressed. Over the years, the behavior moved from what I termed a "happy drunk" to a "mean, vicious, ill-content drunk." The dad we loved was back with us by the time we landed in Oahu after an eight-hour flight. Years later, he told me that he didn't know how long it took the effects to subside, but obviously, that day, the eight hours was enough to sober him up.

We hopped a Hawaiian airline after landing in Oahu over to Maui, where we spent the next seven days in Kaanapali, situated along the northwest side of the island. We looked forward to a relaxing vacation in paradise, but Dad could never sit still, so we found ourselves being dragged from one excursion to another virtually every day. We were grateful for the opportunity to do things that many just dream of, but we weren't able to have as much downtime as we'd hoped. Dad started working on excursions the moment we made it to the Marriott, setting up a full agenda for the week. We were grateful for the pleasure of enjoying a myriad of excursions, but the three of us were guarded and cautious with making suggestions for what we wanted to do, not wanting to upset Dad, as we knew that would lead to us having to endure his wrath.

By the next-to-the-last day, we had fully experienced the island. We had arisen at 3:30 a.m. to venture on an excursion bus to the top of Haleakala to watch the sunrise, riding bikes down the mountain over thirty miles down. It was a breathtaking sunrise and unbelievably cold at the top. We layered on sweatshirts and the yellow "suits" the biking company provided to us, removing layers periodically on the ride down as we reached warmer elevations. On a different day trip, we'd taken a catamaran excursion out to Molokini, where we snorkeled and did modified scuba diving, or as they called it snuba diving. Amazingly, clear waters below provided a view of sea life that reminded you of something you'd see on the Discovery Channel.

We'd spent virtually every night shopping and eating at the wonderful variety of restaurants in Lahaina. Since we had rented a convertible for the week, we also ventured out for the infamous full-day trip on the narrow road to Hana, careening around the winding roads on the northeastern side of the island, ultimately settling in for a picnic lunch at Seven Pools. The pools were formed by waterfalls that cascaded down the side of a mountain, eventually dumping its contents into the ocean. All the while, even during the dangerous drive, Dad had been secretly drinking – nearly nonstop (little did we know) – which made the ride even more . . . adventurous. After becoming sober, the guilt Dad had from this trip and the pain he had put us through over the course of the week was almost unbearable for him. Unfortunately for all of us, his alcoholic behavior would get worse before it got better on this "trip to paradise."

The last day of this trip, we took a puddle jumper back to Oahu, primarily so we could see Pearl Harbor and the International Marketplace. We settled in at the Sheraton on Waikiki Beach, near the Royal Hawaiian, where Mom and Dad had spent most of their honeymoon in '83. When we visited Pearl Harbor, Dad seemed to have the split personality we'd become acquainted with reappear, irritable and gregarious at times, fun-loving and cracking jokes at other times. As most people visiting the sacred site recognize the magnitude of that December day from 1942 that "lives in infamy," the tour of Pearl Harbor was marked by a pronounced quiet reverence, nearly as solemn as a church service when communion is taken.

The only exceptions to that were a handful of Japanese tourists and Dad's loud and obnoxious behavior, all of which seemed out of place at a place where so many Americans lost their lives during the surprise attacks during WWII. It was terribly embarrassing for us, and just one more time, we seemed to not be able to account for Dad's strange behavior, which was becoming more the norm. He wasn't being crude but was just being loud. Ironically, he even pointed out the irreverence of a handful of Japanese tourists. After we made it back to the hotel, we all decided it was time to go relax at the beach, somewhere where Dad's loudness wouldn't stand out, time to go enjoy the famed Waikiki Beach.

Once we made it back at the Sheraton, we packed up our beach paraphernalia, and Dad left us as soon as we got to the beach, claiming he had forgotten something in the room. This was yet another clue for us that we just weren't picking up on, his constant departures for periods of time that resulted in his return in completely different moods. He left and seemed to take a long time for a simple trip to the room and back. I just figured he'd gotten sidetracked or couldn't find whatever he was looking for. That gave me grave fear as I figured he would probably be more irritable when he returned or he might return quite jovial; we never were quite sure who would show up. He confessed to me in later years that he'd made a trip to the ABC Store, where he bought two pints of vodka and had downed both in the hotel restroom before he returned to us. When Dad made it back to the beach, I asked if he found what he was looking for. He looked at me with a questioning look as if he had no clue what I was talking about and then seemed to recall his original lie and said he realized he must have had it with him all along.

He seemed extra relaxed when he got back to the beach, so I thought we had good Dad in our midst again. What a relief. But within the hour, he started yelling at Mom and us for anything and nothing. When he raised his voice, as a general rule, his slur of speech was harder to detect, putting the other person on the defensive. It was twisted, to say the least, and we would feel guilty half the time, displacing what should have been his guilt onto ourselves. Since Dad didn't appear to be drinking anything other than maybe a mixed drink or two at the beach, the whole family continued to dismiss the notion that he might be drunk.

Mom had broached the subject with him on a handful of occasions to which he'd typically fly off the handle and start yelling at her for falsely accusing him of being drunk. This day was one of those occasions, and he looked at her like she had two heads and flatly denied her new allegation of drunkenness yet one more time. Although we still had plenty of daylight left, Mom decided that beach time was over, given the fact that Dad was starting into his tirades yet again. She was simply worn out and didn't want to have to put up with him in a public setting. Lindsey and I were enjoying our time in the ocean, and since we could escape Dad there, both protested when Mom called it a day.

As we packed up our beach belongings and headed back to the hotel room to dress for an early dinner, Dad continued with the verbal abuse with all of us but especially with Mom because of her "false accusation." We somehow had mustered enough energy to get ready for dinner, and Dad disappeared again while everyone was getting ready. He said he needed to check with the front desk to confirm departure information for the next morning since we were heading home. He returned and seemed to be in a good mood once again.

On our way to the restaurant, we ran into a street vendor who Dad decided to engage in a lively conversation. I was thrilled as the person had two beautiful birds perched on his shoulders. One appeared to be a snow-white cockatoo and the other was a brilliantly colored toucan. The birdman's gig was to engage tourists in conversation and then charge for pictures he'd taken with one of those old instant Polaroid cameras, charging $5 apiece for the instant gratification of the pictorial memento. We took four pictures between Lindsey and me and were glad bad Dad had left us, at least for the moment. Based on Mom's disgusted look, she apparently hadn't determined that good Dad was completely back yet. Her premonition was spot on.

We continued toward the restaurant with lifted spirits, but the revolving door of the eating establishment almost seemed to transform good Dad into bad Dad once again. As soon as the hostess told us it would be thirty minutes, he started negotiating with her, and to avoid a scene, she shuffled us into, of all things, the bar for immediate seating. Dad only had one "legal drink," as he later referred to them, during dinner, but he was beyond gone by this time. He gave Mom the look that we were becoming all too familiar with, telling her to never accuse him of being drunk again like she did out on the beach. He even used one of the parenting rules against her that night, an unwritten rule that they agreed to keep these heated "discussions" between the two of them and to never again put him down or accuse him about such things in front of the kids. Talk about calling the kettle black.

The entire dinner was a fiasco from the onset; at times, he'd be despondent, looking off in the distance, and the next moment, he would start into one of us about some trivial thing, like eating with our mouths closed. He called my sister a cow to drive his point about her chomping. I suspect Lindsey never ate with her mouth the slightest bit open after that night, effective but not the place or way to get a child to develop better table manners. None of us ate much that night except Dad who finished every last bite. He kept telling us all to eat, oblivious to the fact we all had completely lost our appetites because of him. He even told Mom that if she ate as light as she did that night all the time, she wouldn't be so fat. Granted, she could have lost a few pounds, but the comment was not only inaccurate but cruel.

Mom finally had her fill and motioned for the waitress to get us the check, which the young lady was more than obliged to do as she wanted Dad out of there as quickly as we wanted to get out of the restaurant. Mom took the bill, handing a credit card back without as much as reviewing the accuracy of the bill. Dad was oblivious to the exchange. Throughout dinner, Dad had made lame attempts to lighten the conversation, and when we didn't respond, he'd rant about something else. The verbal abuse had crossed a line that night, and since it was directed at his family, the restaurant didn't "get involved," but the looks of other patrons at us that night is something I doubt will ever leave my memory bank. Looks of disgust at Dad and looks of pity for the rest of us.

Mom got us out of there, and there was complete silence on the way back to the hotel. Dad walked behind us, which was fine with us. Lindsey and I would turn our heads slightly from time to time on the walk back, checking with our peripheral vision to see if he was still following behind us. I don't know why we were checking as none of us would have cared at that point if he wasn't following us. Mom never looked back as we strode the eight blocks back to the hotel. She shared many years later as we revisited this horrid night that she was praying every step of the walk back that Dad would lose track of us and not be able to find his way back until he found his way back to being good Dad again. It was at this point on this particular evening that she had decided Dad was lost forever, whether he was physically with us or not.

Lindsey and I cried ourselves to sleep that night while Mom tried her best to comfort us, praying with us for Dad. She was being strong for us, but I was able to see her pained face and could almost hear her heart breaking, silently crying herself to sleep with balled up fists, occasionally hitting her pillow in quick, deliberate jabs, much like one would do with a punching bag. My guess was she pictured Dad's face with each quick jab, prayerfully hoping it would displace hurt on him as much as he'd hurt us that night.

We could not understand why he continued to get more abusive over the years and why his demeanor would change at the drop of a hat for what seemed to be no really good reason. He hadn't become physically abusive to us, but we could tell it wasn't far behind the emotional abuse we were already experiencing in heavy doses.

Dad's outburst with us that infamous July night hurt us so deeply that we believed nothing would ever be the same. Not only had he embarrassed us in such a public forum during dinner with his screams of obscenities and belittling all three of us in public, but he seemed to have lost his love for us as family that infamous night. All the while (little did we know) Dad was in a blackout the entire evening. He would not remember any part of that day beyond the beach time in the afternoon.

He awoke the next morning in a relatively good mood, asking us if we were ready to end our "trip to paradise." Our stunned faces in response to his question that morning must have spoken volumes to him. He looked at us in a questioning look, quickly realizing that he must have ticked us off or something the night before. He sheepishly stated that he was sorry for last night with no specifics cited, all because he couldn't recall the specifics of that dreadful night. What he didn't realize with his lackluster apology was the magnitude of damage to the family this time around. His simple apology was not going to suffice. Based on our silence, he could sense that he'd crossed a line this time that would not easily be forgiven.

To say we were petrified of him by this point was an understatement. We didn't know what he might do or say or what might set him off, so silence and withdrawal became our protection. Dad told me after he got sober about the number and degree of blackouts he was having during those days. Not only did I not understand but doubted seriously that anyone had lapses of memory to this degree. After his years of sobriety and reading about alcoholism, I finally became convinced that blackouts must be real and time lapses are not uncommon for a drunk. Even when Dad saw the pictures of Lindsey and I with the birds after the trip, he asked when we had those pictures taken. He had no memory of our time with the birdman. It is still painful to us, but we now knew that Dad had episodes of blackouts throughout our Hawaii trip, and evidently, he was in one most of our last full day on Oahu. There were specific events during the trip that I'd later test his memory. Based on his recollection of events, Dad's memory card appeared to be partially erased, regardless; the blackouts became more frequent and lasted longer as his drinking career advanced.

Mom told us a few years later that on the long flight home, she was praying that the plane would crash, so we would no longer have to live in this crazy life that had seemed to have spiraled out of control. She didn't believe in divorce but couldn't see continuing life as it was at this point, still not knowing what was happening to the husband she had married. This was not the same man. She even wondered if he might have a brain tumor that might be impacting his behavior, a sign of things to come, but not the issue at this point in time.

After the Hawaiian vacation fiasco, Mom had full intentions of packing the three of us up and moving back to St. Louis to live with her parents, leaving Dad to be on his own, until (and if) he could figure out what was wrong with him. Her intent was a separation to wake him up. These plans hadn't been shared with Dad yet, but Mom had prepared Lindsey and me the night we got home, and by this point, though still confused, were both in agreement with the plan. Our father was transforming into someone we no longer wanted to be around. We were fearful of him as his behavior had become more and more erratic and unpredictable. Would we have good Dad or bad Dad today? That had gotten to be a consistent question in our minds, fearful of which Greg Bagwell we would encounter on any given day or moment, for that matter. A real-life Jekyll and Hyde in our midst, embodied in the being of our own father.

According to what we learned a few years later, when Mom confronted him to have a serious conversation the day after we returned home from the vacation, Dad had agreed. Finally realizing that his addiction was real and that he had lost all control, he had already made up his mind that he was going to expose his big dark secret. However, even that confession came with strings attached. He told Mom that her reaction to what he was about to tell her would determine how well he would get through this, trying to place his recovery clearly in her hands. Apparently, these guilt trips that addicts put others on are not unusual, basing their performance on how others react to and deal with them. He told her he was sick and tired of the person that he'd become, that it wasn't fair to her or his children, adding that he finally had come to the realization that he was an alcohol and drug abuser. This news blew her away as it wasn't what she expected, nor was it overtly obvious that he was a substance abuser.

She knew he would have a drink from time to time but didn't expect this confession since she'd never seen him have more than two or three drinks, tops. Sure, she knew his behavior had become totally unpredictable and erratic but was honestly surprised that this was the issue. Even with her periodic suspicions, she had trusted his denials and dismissed them as her mind playing games on her. He was hiding liquor and drugs, only having his "legal" drink or two in public. Mom later told us that she felt as if her life hit a rewind button that day, which took her back through a series of issues and times in their lives that vaguely started to make sense as she replayed the tape of their recent past in her mind.

It took years for the damage that was done to heal in our family. Mom demanded, upon Dad's confession, that he get professional help immediately or she would pack up immediately and move the three of us in with her parents in St. Louis. She was not about to allow him to place the responsibility of his recovery in her hands. This was his issue, and he needed to deal with it. Lindsey and I were brought into the loop about his substance abuse a couple of days later over dinner.

Dad could barely get the words out during his confession over dinner, sobbing and apologizing for not dealing with the issue earlier. He focused on the disease and nearly blamed his genetic makeup completely for his disease since there were a number of alcoholics in his family. Lindsey and I felt sorry for the broken man we saw before us that night. We forgave him immediately and looked forward to helping him get well, knowing we would do anything to help and support him through his recovery process. He obviously couldn't do this on his own, and we made a pact to make ourselves available to him through his healing, even though we were ill-equipped to get an addict on the road to recovery. It's amazing how those who are most impacted by addicts seem to think the only one that needs fixing is the addict; we needed as much recovery and healing as he did.

The day Dad came clean with the truth, he fulfilled the commitment he'd made to Mom and called an alcohol abuse hotline. He admitted himself for rehab for a thirty-day outpatient program, which would start the day after his phone call. Inpatient care was out of the question as his pride and ego couldn't handle anyone finding out that he was an addict. The outpatient program combined with a step program, and he seemed well on his way to recovery by the end of the second week in treatment. Fast forward ten years and after multiple relapses, which were getting harder for him to cover up from us, and he finally had strung three years together. The step programs had helped him get sober, but he fully gave the credit to staying sober to God, not some obscure higher power as the sustaining strength and power he needed in his battle with substance abuse.

He understood that relying on his own strength and power didn't work, and Dad truly relied on his higher power. His routine was first thing in the morning to ask God to be his power and strength for the day over addiction for the current twenty-four hours and thanking Him at night for sobriety for just one more day, in addition to becoming more grounded in his faith. Learning from the past, not projecting too far into the future, having accountability partners, and staying in the current twenty-four hours seemed to be a winning formula that finally worked. Based on his success in battling his addiction demons to date and the unbelievable transformation in this man who I now respected, and I wasn't about to dispute his formula, it was working!

Lindsey and I had wished so desperately that Mom could have had more years with "new Dad." Not that the road to recovery was free of bumps and potholes. It seemed to us that she got cheated the most out of all of us, though, but she wasn't complaining these days. The addiction was not the only thing that needed work. Their marriage and relationship was damaged and needed help as well due to years of lies and addictive behaviors. After finally conceding to biblical counseling after at least two failed rounds of marriage counseling and years of focus on addiction recovery, they were doing so well now that we could finally put the painful past behind us. The past would always be there, but we came to the realization that one must learn from the past, never close the door on it, but focus on the here and now, relishing every moment.

Mom and Dad were truly becoming what I believed God had intended for all married couples to be – filled with love. They even had the opportunity to celebrate their twenty-fifth anniversary in Saint Lucia in October, less than two months ago. Dad even sprung for renewal of vows through the resort, surprising Mom with what evidently was in many ways more meaningful than their original marriage ceremony, from what they had described. Their relationship was obviously on more solid footing, and at times, they acted more like newlyweds than a midlife couple, as I so affectionately called them these days.

Mom was typically so soft-spoken, but as of late, she seemed to want us to know how well she and Dad were doing. A few times, she'd mentioned how good their "alone times" were. She knew we'd react with "Mom . . . please . . . too much information," followed by covering our ears with both hands, walking out of the room or chanting, "La la la la," so we wouldn't hear more. The stark reality was that both Lindsey and I were delighted to hear that they were becoming more like one flesh every day. It beat the heck out of not knowing which Dad was going to be with us on any given day and whether Mom was going to be angry or depressed and despondent for the day. Our lives had been a series of mountaintops and valleys, and though many wouldn't consider it to be that with all our current set of circumstances, we considered this particular time a mountaintop. Realizing one still has a view of the valley once on a mountaintop, being out of the valley was so freeing, and the view of life was much more spectacular. We'd grown so accustomed to drama and chaos in the home, though, from years of a parent in addiction that we almost didn't know how to deal with calmness and serenity, something I'd heard wasn't unfamiliar to children of addicts.

We were wishing Mom could be with us today, but she was entertaining her family, half of which had just made it in town from St. Louis and Boston this afternoon. Dad insisted that she spend time with them and warm them up to the idea of the upcoming funeral, which was planned to take place this Saturday.

Already Wednesday, I could see that this was going to move way too quickly; it seemed so surreal and final to us with the funeral only three short days away.

# CHAPTER 4

"OK, SHERRI, WE'RE here to support you and know Greg is more than a little eccentric, which is becoming more apparent every day," Sherri's dad, Al, said this lovingly to his youngest, still feeling the need to protect his baby. "But I'm really not getting this whole 'funeral before the funeral' deal. Are we gonna be back again in two months for the 'real deal'?"

With an almost audible laugh and sigh, Sherri addressed the whole group, rather than just her father. "Dad, Mom, this will be the one and only funeral. There will not be another one, and at Greg's request, only the immediate family is invited to the 'real deal,' as you call it. He plans on being cremated, and Lindsey, Jared, and I already have exact instruction on where to spread his ashes . . . a handful of places that he's requested."

Grandma Bender, trying to be sensitive but also trying to understand, asked, "Sherri, sweetie, I know it's the eleventh hour, but can't we just talk Greg into a more traditional process here. I love him like my own son, but it just seems to me that this is going to be . . ." – she hesitated to say it, then continuing – "Well . . . very uncomfortable for all of us to endure." Grandma Bender could best be described as a proper Midwest woman of great morals and all about formality and proper processes. She didn't like anything out of the norm, and Dad's request for the service was beyond her comfort zone.

"Mom, I assure you that the details are well laid out, and we're all to be there and act like Greg isn't even there. It will be fine. I'm actually looking forward to it now, and trust me when I say I blew a gasket when he first mentioned it to me. But now, it's making more sense as I understand why Greg has planned this funeral event while he's still with us. It will be anything but traditional. It'll be fine, trust us."

Sherri knew she wouldn't be able to sell most of her current audience on the funeral experience Greg had chosen, but she fully trusted Greg and desired more than anything to fulfill this last request. Knowing a couple of the details that others didn't know gave her even greater comfort at the thought of the coming event. She simply grinned and closed her eyes, even with her family sitting nearby and still talking among themselves. She was at peace, a peace beyond all understanding, a peace that only could come from above.

"Table for two, please."

The young lady behind the hostess station pulled two menus from a holder on the side of the podium, ready to seat us with no wait. "Right this way." The hostess smiled and turned, walking away, fully expecting us to be following her. We didn't disappoint her and followed her to our table.

Dad was looking at me with a sideways glance that spoke volumes without words en route to our table. His head slowly bobbing up and down, and he had that grin on his face that was shouting out to me in silence, "She's cute. She's interested in you, so get her phone number!" Knowing Dad, he would always add, "Provided she was a fully sold out Christian." I could have cared less about the latter. After all, she was cute and obviously was interested in me if her flirtatious looks were being read right. No ego problem here.

As we were settling into our booth, I heard a shriek that I'd recognize anywhere from the other side of the restaurant. I turned in the general direction of what not only was drawing our attention but half the people in the restaurant. Most eyes met her eyes and slowly gravitated downward to what absolutely couldn't be hidden anymore. The round belly, which obviously held a baby. Lindsey was gleefully hopping from foot to foot by now and getting closer with her arms held straight out for Grandpa Bagwell.

Dad just beamed, realizing he was about to have not only another meal with his son but with his daughter and "son-in-love" (as Mom called him) as well.

"Dad, you look great!"

"And you look . . . radiant. You glow. You look like you should be floating out of one of those fabric commercials in a sea of billowy, puffy white clouds. Have no clue what billowy is, but it sounds good!" Dad said this swaying with flailing arms to emphasize the visual as he stepped toward and embraced his oldest child.

By this time, my cheeks were turning red from embarrassment as we'd clearly become a center of attention for the patrons at Dave's. "Guys, you're like really embarrassing me. Can we just sit down? I'm sure they won't mind if you join us. I have a feeling I might just have an inroad with the hostess too, if we need it." I glanced over and noted my new hostess friend, who had a broad, approving smile plastered on her face. As our eyes met, she waved a menu toward us with a look that said, "It's OK," indicating that we could invite our guests to join us at our oversized booth to break bread.

John had already quietly slid into the booth, knowing that Lindsey and Dad needed their moment. "This is too cool," he said as he motioned at the group with his arms outstretched and palms open in an approving manner.

"Can you believe we ended up in the same place tonight?" Dad's smile said it all, but he added a phrase for emphasis that this was not a mere coincidence. "Now *that* is a God thing!" That bold statement had become a regular phrase we expected from Dad whenever he was trying to make a point that there really was no such thing as coincidence. I'd had to take the word 'coincidence' out of my vocabulary as I knew Dad would try to convince me about God's sovereignty and how there are no coincidences. Blah, blah, blah. It finally got so old that I conceded to him, trying to consciously take the 'coincidence' word out of spoken vocabulary, at least around Dad.

John chimed in with complete agreement in his voice. "You got that right, Pops. It's definitely a God thing!" He quickly toned down his enthusiasm, however, as he looked over at my sister, whose mood appeared to be changing quickly from thrilled to near sadness. I just marked it up to pregnancy hormonal imbalance. That's not what it was.

Sheepishly, Lindsey made a sincere but reluctant-sounding offer at this point. "Dad, whatever you want tonight is on us, right, Johnny Boy?" Unsure if the offer to pay for our meals or using the name for her husband that our mother used for my brother-in-law caught him more by surprise but John quickly tried to conceal his confusion at Lindsey's mood shift and offer made on his behalf with an "Absolutely!"

It was so easy to drift back in thought during moments like this night when just Dad and us kids were out to dinner, enjoying each other's company immensely, laughing and carrying on to the point that you knew all eyes were on us, but who cared, right? In times past, it could have been that Dad's zeal and enthusiasm was actually the result of his alcohol and drug "highs" or just a subconscious way of "getting under the skin of our mother." During those months of separation from Mom, whether they lived together under the same roof or not, we knew we'd have a good time with Dad but had no idea during times past that there were major issues below the surface that were disguised behind the funhouse we always seemed to be in when it was just us.

Our new and improved Dad, although still a life of the party, carried it off now with a fun, calm reassurance to those around him, and it never failed; he always brought up the God stuff. I was certainly OK with the God stuff, knowing I'd rather him be high on spiritual things rather than the booze and drugs. Although he wouldn't lie to us if we asked a direct question about his abuse, he also didn't proactively talk about the painful past. I knew he had learned from the past and didn't shut the door on it, but he also didn't drive forward in life by staring at the rearview mirror. That was my mom's specialty, though, for a number of years after Dad's first attempt at sobriety; she seemed to not be able to look anywhere but the rearview mirror of life, and that caused a strife between the two of them that finally got to a point that we were "rejoicing" (to use one of Dad's terms) when the two of them separated for five months the previous year. It was hard to believe they'd come so close to hanging it up.

"Jared... Hello... Are you in there?" Lindsey knocked in midair, getting my attention and helping to bring me back into reality and their conversation. It seemed to her like I was in a distant place in my mind and needed to get in the here and now. She was right. I shook my head and shoulders, flailing my arms about as if that would transform me into the here and now, and it seemed to work.

Dad knew me like a book and had already ordered for me while I was drifting off to thoughts of the past, and our salads were already being placed in front of us. *Yep, you know me well, Dad.* Honey mustard dressing on the side and loads of fresh ground pepper to the point that you have as much black as green showing on the salad. I was taking my first forkful when Dad said, "Woe, guys. Let's bless our food and our time together this evening." We always prayed together over meals no matter where the meal was being served, and we weren't about to stop that tradition tonight.

"Dear Father in heaven, you are most awesome in all the universe, and we praise you for all you have done, continue to do, and will do in our future here on earth and in heaven. Bless this food and the hands that prepared it." This last part was followed by a chuckle from the entire group as this was an inside joke with our immediate family. Blessing hands that prepared the meal had originally been something reserved for Mom at home, but it evolved over time as an extra blessing to whoever was preparing our meal. When at restaurants, we all tried to picture who we were blessing that had prepared our food. It got pretty funny at times when we would describe the chef that had prepared our food. "Father, we love you and thank you for directing our footpaths to this location together this evening so we can enjoy one more time together, making new memories for each of us that we treasure, and we love you. In Jesus's name . . ." An intentional pause, followed by a unanimous amen from all four of us, closed out our prayer.

We were all ready to enjoy our meal together and another of those times of joy as a family, but without Mom this time. At least, I thought that's how the evening would play out. But Lindsey just kept staring at Dad with tears forming in her eyes, taking in every moment, holding her stomach as if caressing her unborn child, knowing we didn't have many times like this left with this "man of God" we called Dad. Realizing that her seriousness and intensity were bound to be a downer for the group, she blinked her eyes several times, blew out air, and determined to join in the fun.

The remainder of our dinner was enveloped with love and laughter, recounting memories of days gone by. Given the fact that Lindsey was about to become a mother, Dad shared stories that night about early parenthood, recounting how inept he and Mom felt with a newborn in the house. He shared one of my favorite stories about a time Mom greeted him at the front door when Dad returned after a hard day's work. She was still in her nightgown and looked pretty disheveled, according to Dad. She handed six-month-old Lindsey over to him before he had a chance to get any further than the foyer in an obviously nonverbal way to say she was done for the day with the infant. Dad was fine with that, well, under normal circumstances.

He adored his baby girl and was thrilled with spending time holding her, feeding her, playing with her, and just loving on her. But this particular day, she had been beyond fussy due to an extreme case of diarrhea. As mentioned, upon Dad's arrival home and just entering the entry hallway, Mom met him with baby in tow, handing her off before he had a chance to debate or contest. She had a concise, simple message: There was a mess in the baby's room, and he needed to clean it up since she was spent. "And oh yeah, here's *your* child," she added.

He proceeded to tell us how he walked into the baby room expecting a mess but had no idea what he was in for. He described having to clean the wall above the changing table, wondering how the law of physics worked to have such a mess as far as two feet above the table and on the wall, of all things. No major complaints from Dad, but Mom did overhear him in the nursery, telling Lindsey that they'd gotten rid of a dog for doing less than this. We all laughed at the story, knowing Dad didn't have the heart to get rid of a dog, let alone his daughter, for what must have been a disgusting mess. Dad became the "clean up guy" every time from that point forward whenever any of us were sick while Mom served the role of comforter and caterer to our needs. Roles must be defined early into parenthood, and theirs were defined that day for our sick days to come.

# CHAPTER 5

THE NEXT MORNING, I awoke at the lake house to the smells of bacon, homemade biscuits, and bold coffee. I knew there was more than that spread out in the formal dining room, which typically seated about a dozen comfortably. Mom loved entertaining, and knowing her, the fine china would be out, and it would look more like a Christmas feast than a Thursday morning breakfast with a few relatives in from out of town. I wasn't the only one waking up to the smells and sizzling sounds because I heard my mom's brother, Gail, and his wife, Cindy, talking quietly as they freshened up in the Jack-and-Jill bathroom, which was situated between my room and Lindsey's old room.

The lake house (as we called it) was Mom and Dad's primary residence for the past ten years, situated on a beautifully landscaped two-acre sloping lot next to a ten-acre lake. The lake was surrounded by dense woods on all sides. The woods made the lot so private that you couldn't see neighbors spring through fall with all the foliage and trees. The cedar and stone home had a real eye appeal from the curb with all its depth and angles which included multiple gabled areas, a number of dormers atop, and a large two-story turret on one end, which looked somewhat out of place on the rather country-looking home. One of my favorite parts of the home was the three-sided wrap-around porch, fully equipped with multiple porch swings and sitting areas all around, plenty of areas to get away from it all and read a good book or just relax, which I'd done both often in the serene setting. The atmosphere at the home was that of a retreat, which was exactly what the Bagwell's were looking for when they went house hunting eleven years ago.

We had moved from Naperville, which had been voted most kid-friendly city in the United States during our time there. Much loved in this southwestern city to Chicago were the conveniences of restaurants, shopping, and the easy thirty-five-minute commute downtown for Dad's job, but Mom and Dad had a desire to get away from the hustle and bustle. Dad had spent his high school days in the small town of Bald Knob, Arkansas, where his mom and dad had both retired due to disability just before his dad died from renal kidney failure. He loved the openness of living on twenty acres of land in their very rural homestead in Bald Knob. Their property contained spring-fed streams and natural ponds, which provided Dad the ability to fish or hunt at a moment's notice. a virtual retreat in the most laid-back of atmospheres.

So during the three-year stint in Naperville, Dad maintained a strong desire for his family to be able to experience retreat-like living for us as well, which he couldn't picture anywhere in the burbs of Chicagoland. Mom was the one who encouraged their search, which proved to be more productive than either of them believed possible. For starters, postage-size lots in Naperville were going for well over $100,000 during the late '90s, and for any amount of acreage, you were looking at well over $500,000, and that didn't include the dwelling. So they started looking in what few rural areas were left in the small towns west of and north of Naperville, areas that were still fairly open and sparsely populated.

Mom had hoped that a move to the "country" would help them start afresh, praying that Dad's severe mood swings and general irritability that had become the norm would change with a fresh, new environment as well. Surroundings wasn't Dad's problem, though, and he took himself and his "issues" with him to our newfound home in the small town of Hampshire, Illinois, where we finally found the perfect place. The town was a throwback to a bygone era when we moved "out there" ten years ago, many large farms and a small old main street with two-story turn-of-the-century buildings that all had seen better days and a handful of diners that hadn't changed much since the 1960s.

Hampshire didn't even have a stoplight, just a "stop and go" light at Main Street and Route 72, the primary intersection of the town. The "stop and go" light blinked a constant flashing red, and beside it on the main drag was (and still is) the Chick and Dip, a small local burger, chicken, and ice cream joint. We grew to love the broasted chicken, homemade slaw, and those ice-cream delicacies from the Chick and Dip; it became a routine stop during the long days of summer. Sitting out under the awning on the picnic tables added to the ambiance of the place. All that was missing were servers on roller skates and a row of '50s Chevrolets. On occasion, they'd sponsor an "oldies" night, which inevitably would turn the parking lot into a virtual scene from *American Graffiti*.

All the charm of small-town America, with the promise of suburbia in the years to come, Hampshire was the ideal place that our family was seeking. Schools were a concern of Mom's, though, as the public schools weren't nearly as well rated as the highly acclaimed public schools in Naperville. She had researched and compared IGAP scores between the two sets of public schools that we attended and would potentially attend, telling us that the little town's public schools were behind in every category except math. In my ten short years of life at that point, I'd already developed a confidence bordering on cockiness and told her and Dad that I could help them get their IGAP scores up, and I was serious, and they knew it. Even though Mom was a product of the private school system, she and Dad did agree on one thing: We should attend public schools.

One of the reasons they felt so strongly about public school attendance was the services that Lindsey and I received, due to our hearing impairment, in the public school system. We received speech therapy, modified testing, and preferential seating, among other things to ensure we were mainstreamed, not only into the school, but into life in general. We also had special people made available to us called hearing itinerants, who were floaters within a school district that became our voice in the public school system. There were a couple of planned meetings per year scheduled with our teachers in which parents, teachers, and the itinerant attended, discussing challenges, issues, and progress. Many of these sessions were emotional for Mom as she wanted the best for her babies, as she'd called us till way after when we were out of diapers. I suspect Dad was half lit for more than half of those meetings, which might have had an impact on

Mom's emotional state during those meetings as well. Regardless, the school system decided by the time I was in sixth grade that I no longer qualified for the services, which was fine by me. I detested being pulled out of class as it made me "different," a word I learned to hate early on in life.

The Hampshire home in the "country" (better known as the Lake House) had five bedrooms and an attached self-contained apartment, as we called it, with another bedroom, bath, kitchenette, laundry, living area, and separate entrance. If that didn't make enough room, there was a finished basement with full bath and Murphy bed, which provided more than sufficient room when hosting out-of-town guests or just a group of kids for a sleepover when Lindsey and I were younger. Mom and Dad insisted on out-of-towners staying at the house and would put out cots or sleeping bags and even a tent outside during pleasant weather for the youngsters. All so the family could be together.

Everyone seemed to enjoy the "Bagwell Inn," except Dad's brother, Gene, who insisted on staying at a hotel when visiting. I wasn't quite sure why he did that but knew that he and Dad had grown somewhat distant in the years since Dad had straightened out his life. I knew they loved each other, but maybe Gene got his fill of the God talk around the house and just didn't want to see and hear about it 24-7. I could relate to that, but for now, knowing the limited time we had with Dad, I could endure it. One thing was for certain, our home had never been a showcase, but truly more like a retreat, and most everyone who visited felt a warmth and welcome second to none. I attributed that to Mom, the proverbial and gracious hostess. She had quite a decorating flair but didn't leave one with the feeling that they were walking onto a page of a Home and Garden's layout.

At this point, I heard Mom quietly and matter-of-factly giving Dad instruction on what he needed to do to help prepare breakfast for the house guests. I wasn't eavesdropping but guess the new digital technology of my hearing aids were working fairly well, especially when I turned up the volume. OK, so maybe I was eavesdropping. I could almost visualize the scene in the kitchen without even being in the room, something I figured would become normal for me at some point in the future. Not realizing that any of us could hear her soft word, Sherri Bagwell was reprimanding Greg Bagwell, and I could see it in my mind's eye, his arms wrapped around her and kissing her softly on the back of her neck and moving around to a point that Mom would have died if she'd even thought that any of us had seen them in this position. I had more than once, little did she know.

"Greg," softly she called his name. "You stop that right this minute." She laughed or moaned or both. "We're gonna get caught, and it'll be your fault."

"Who cares. Let 'em find us like this. At least, they'll know how much I love you, Martha, or is it Mary." I had no idea what he meant by those nicknames but remember something about a Bible story I'd heard when I was a kid, a story in which Jesus actually sided with one of the two of these ladies. Interestingly enough, as I recall from the story, Jesus seemed to come to the defense of the lady (Martha or Mary, whichever it was) that was just sitting around, visiting with Him, and not the one that was working her tail off. Not sure I understood the point of that story or Dad's implication but felt they were related.

"Gregory Wayne, that's it. You cease this instant!" They were so predictable, and though I wouldn't want them to know my thoughts, I actually thought they were amazingly cute together. Mom must have convinced Dad to stop with his playfulness as she now was humming, and I heard the single high-pitched beep of the alarm system go off, indicating Dad must have gone outside or into the garage.

As I closed my eyes, I could visualize Mom, smiling with her shoulder-length brunette hair up in a loose bun, attired in a modest but becoming nightgown, busying herself around the kitchen. She was humming some contemporary Christian tune that seemed vaguely familiar. I tried to place the tune that she was humming, something, I think, about an awesome God, and as I thought about it, it had been around for years and probably not considered contemporary at this point in time. Regardless, I adored hearing Mom's humming and singing around the house, feeling her content state that seemed to set a peaceful, serene atmosphere in our home.

So much better than the days when she moped around in what seemed to be a depressed state in years past. During those dark years, she was just trying to hold it together and protect us from knowing the dysfunction that had become our lives. She became an invisible protective shield for us, and as far as we could tell for years, we had a "normal" home life. Knowing what I knew now about those years, I realize that Mom was a woman of character, a Godly woman, and a supermom who kept our lives somewhat together during very uncertain times in our past, keeping us from having to endure the nightmare she was living in with an addict.

As she continued moving from the kitchen, I sensed that she was in that contagiously positive mood, virtually waltzing, or at least, frolicking with that seemingly permanent smile on her pale, but beautiful china-doll-like face. I heard clanking of silverware, knowing she was putting the finishing touches on the dining room table. I never understood how she did it, but she always made our home so inviting and never made guests or family feel uncomfortable due to pomp or circumstance. Casual elegance, I'd heard someone term her "style." Sounded good to me. All I knew was Mom was the perfect hostess. I felt like Dad had married the most patient and gracious woman in the world. A contemporary June Cleaver, with a hint of Martha Stewart and Mother Teresa, all wrapped up in one unbelievable woman I was proud to call Mom. Oh, she had her faults, but these days, you really had to dig or nitpick to find them, really!

As I quietly descended the steps downstairs in my collegiate-looking pajamas, which included Chicago Bears bottoms of blue and orange and a basic blue V-neck T-shirt, Mom was still able to hear me from the other side of the house. To say I'm not a morning person is an understatement, and from an appearance standpoint, I might even be viewed as a naturalist. No brushing my long, naturally curly dark mop of hair, just a simple quick turn of my head and running my fingers through it once for good measure. No brushing of teeth, but a quick gargle of mouthwash, so I didn't offend anyone with that horrific morning breath. Even when I did "get ready" at some point in the day to spend fifteen minutes between the shower, shave, and putting on my clothes would be considered a long time. If I would have ever spent an hour getting ready like my sister, somebody in the family probably would have called 911.

"Jared, is that you?" awaiting a split second for a response from me. Since I wasn't quick enough. "Bud, I need your help. Can you make another pot of coffee?" Mom had acute hearing while Dad had selective hearing. Not at all sure how that genetic thing worked since Lindsey and me both were born with moderate to severe hearing loss. Go figure.

The discovery of the hearing loss of sis and I seemed to be the catalyst that would forever change our lives. Up until that point, our immediate family appeared to be what most would have described as fairy-tale-like existence. Dad just couldn't deal with the stark reality of our hearing impairment, and he found his "escape from feeling" in alcohol and drugs, changing our perfect little lives, as some would have termed it, many years back, long before Lindsey or I had any knowledge of the fact we were the products of a dysfunctional family. From what Dad has told me within the past few years, the loss he felt when he found out about our hearing loss was more devastating to him than the loss of either parent. He said that I'd understand that more when I became a father, stating that a parent is most vulnerable with anything that impacts their child. I think I get that even now, though parenthood is way out there for me.

# CHAPTER 6

MOM HAD SUSPECTED that Lindsey had some issue with hearing when she was just fourteen months old. The first cues were delayed speech, aggressive behavioral issues, combined with her lack of consistent response with Mom to oral commands. This was refuted, however, when an audiologist in Germantown, Tennessee (our home in the late '80s) confirmed through testing with an outcome that Lindsey had perfect hearing and that she and Dad just had a hardheaded child. "Up discipline with the kid. Obviously, she's misbehaving and needs more discipline," he urged, to which Dad and Mom obliged.

The Christmas before Lindsey's third birthday, the Bagwell clan made the trek to St. Louis for their every-other-year holiday visit with the Benders, Mom's parents. The visit also drew both sets of Mom's brothers and sisters-in-law along with their set of three kids each, all of which were from out of town, quite a houseful, and even though they enjoyed getting together as a complete family, the trips were fraught with challenges for Mom and Dad. It seemed that the one of the younger cousins, my sister, Lindsey, was constantly getting into trouble with the other cousins. Mom and Dad were convinced that the entire family just figured they had no clue on parenting based on their unruly, aggressive youngster.

That Christmas, Dad started to really study and pay attention to Lindsey's behavioral issues, which seemed to be only slightly improving. They'd started speech therapy for Lindsey about a year earlier due to her delayed speech and even put her in preschool a couple of days a week so she'd have interaction with other kids. The thought was that she'd calm down and learn to better interact with other children, even in basic behavior such as sharing. The three-day-a-week speech therapy seemed to have moderate results at best, still not quite bringing her up to par with her peer group in regards to communication skills. In Dad's evaluation of Lindsey that Christmas away from home, he noticed that Lindsey wouldn't respond to him when he'd call for her, whether trying to stop her from additional misbehavior with the senior cousins or otherwise. And when she did notice he was talking or yelling at her, she would come up close to him to listen and respond accordingly. Little did he know at that time but she was reading his lips, which was a skill set that both Lindsey and I learned early on as a way to receive communication.

When our family returned home to Tennessee after this particular visit, Dad told Mom that he was suspicious that there really was some kind of hearing issue with their daughter. Even though confused based on prior assessment, he convinced Mom that they go back to have her rechecked at the audiologist office. Although he was the first to accept the audiologist's original diagnosis that there was no hearing issue, he now doubted the results, which Mom never seemed willing to accept from the onset. He had told Mom to drop her doubting months earlier as she would bring up periodically that there still seemed to be a hearing issue, even though they'd gotten a clear diagnosis that there was no hearing issue. Call it mother's instinct or the fact that Mom spent more time with Lindsey as a stay-at-home mom, but Mom was right all along.

They were able to get into the same audiologist within a few days of their return to the Memphis area for a recheck, one day before Lindsey's third birthday. Since they refused to believe a manual test in the booth, they demanded that a more fail-proof test be completed. After the electrodes were attached to Lindsey's tiny, blonde curly head, the doctor began to read the results and almost instantaneously had a confused and concerned look on his face. Obviously, the doc was not a poker player, or at least not a good one.

"What is it?" Dad and Mom asked, almost in unison.

"This seems inconsistent with prior test results, but it looks as though your daughter has moderate to severe hearing loss," the doctor told them, very matter of factly.

"Do what?" Mom asked, more in the form of a confused statement, trying to understand. Dad just sat in silent shock and utter disbelief. Before the audiologist could respond to Mom, his nurse, who was flipping through Lindsey's records, gasped, "Oh my gosh, no . . . I . . ."

"What?"

"This previous test in Lindsey's file . . . It isn't her audiology results." Being a small office, she walked over to a group of files, and lo and behold, she pulled another child's records, and there were Lindsey's records plain as day in another child's files, where they'd been for the past eighteen months.

There was a commotion and a surreal feeling to what was happening in the office. The audiologist and the nurse were conferring with each other with backs turned, but there was no hiding the error. They both turned toward Mom and Dad with pursed lips, trying to come up with words to not only ease the pain of what they were learning but to erase their own error in some way that wouldn't come across as a cover-up for the mistake.

Mom's first reaction was sadness because of the increased discipline both parents had administered over the past eighteen months. Both were in disbelief. Dad shifted from disbelief and almost immediately into anger, wanting to know what his daughter had been hearing the first three years of her life.

"Put me in the sound booth!" he demanded, not even trying to be polite at this point. "I want to know what my child has been hearing the first three years of her life!"

"I don't think that's a good idea," the audiologist said, trying to quietly, without explanation, convince Dad that this really was probably the worst idea and not beneficial to anyone present.

"I want to know! I'm going in the booth now, and I want to hear what Lindsey hears. Now!"

They reluctantly obliged, closing the door to the soundproof glass-encased testing booth, which Dad had already entered. Dad quickly took a seat in the lone chair in the small room, which faced a window out into the open room. Without instruction, he had already put on the headphones required for the tests conducted in the booth. The audiologist talked to him to ensure he could hear him, still unconvinced this was a good idea. Dad sternly responded, obviously not backing down to proceed, "Yes, I hear you."

While turning the volume down slowly and deliberately, he said, "I am turning the volume down to the level that Lindsey hears at . . ." His voice disappeared slowly, and Dad could barely understand but a handful of the words that were being spoken to him by the time the volume was at Lindsey's level of hearing.

Dad lost it that day in the soundproof testing booth. Life seemed to drain from his face, and he screamed out with fists raised, looking as if he might implode. Even with the soundproofing of the booth, Mom and the audiologist were able to hear him with no problem. Mom just sat, holding her baby girl, feeling an overwhelming sense of guilt and hopelessness. Mom got through the worst part of the grieving process within the next few months, focusing her energies on Lindsey. But this was the beginning of a spiral that took Dad to the depths of hell on earth, angry at God, especially when his prayers for healing of this sweet, innocent child weren't "answered." His grief and anger would last for years.

As Dad knew the effects of alcohol when he, on occasion, had had a little bit too much to drink, he found solace and escape from the pain that he couldn't face alone in the bottle. His escape to the bottle came quickly, just a day or two after the confirmation of Lindsey's hearing impairment. Alcohol had become his new best friend. Vodka became his alcohol of choice due to its reduced detectability on the breath. He quickly became a closet drinker and, what he'd self-proclaimed later in his disease, a functional alcoholic, who really could control it. The drugs didn't come back until later when the alcohol wasn't working for him any longer as a way to dull his senses, so he wouldn't have to feel what life seemed to unfairly dish out to him.

# CHAPTER 7

"MOM-A-SAN," I SAID, using another of the many bad imitations of other nationalities. "I here at yo service," I said as I bowed in reverence to the master hostess, with hands pressed together as if praying. She just laughed and threw a dish towel at me in jest. We grew up in a house where there really was no prejudice, and I suppose that helped us justify our imitations of others. We certainly meant no harm, but others who didn't know us might think we were poking fun at those who spoke in broken or colloquial English. We considered anything other than a midwestern accent fair game. In reality, we believed the midwestern accent to be the absence of accent. After all, didn't most broadcasters train in the Midwest to remove any detection of an accent? That's what we'd always heard and stood by that as a fact that we had no accent. Reality was that everyone has an accent when they're not amidst their own geography. Oh well.

"Yes, my son." Mom joined me, trying to continue our little game in character. "You go far in life, if you so choose to assist matronly figure of household with acts of service and kindness. Coffee filter in cabinet, below coffee maker." At this, she laughed at herself, even though it was a lame attempt at her accent of the Orient. Since she made the attempt, though, I acknowledged it with an 'hmmm' laugh, so as not to encourage her to continue with this particular charade of sorts, but rewarding her nonetheless.

Once everyone arrived at the table a short time later, breakfast started off a little tentative, but Dad had a knack for making people comfortable during uncomfortable circumstances. This meal with Mom's family was no different.

"So Pops." Dad called Grandpa Bender Pops as far back as I could recall. "You want to know why this funeral service is going to be so perfect?"

As if he had been asked a question that really didn't need to be asked, Grandpa B said "Uh . . . Well . . . I'm sure you've thought this through, son . . . and have your reasons for doing this before it's time."

To which Dad let out a slight laugh. "Well, let me help rest everyone's mind as to what the format will be, why we're having it in a theater, and how our Lord most high will be exalted as a result of this service. The only ones I hope are uncomfortable with this service are those who are not 100 percent absotively, posilutely sure of their salvation. Here's what I envision . . ." As he proceeded to lay out the master plan, I discretely left since I knew it would get overly religious from this point forward with Dad, who couldn't stop talking about his excitement for the next life and the upcoming funeral service he'd planned. Dad seemed not just comfortable with death but seemed to look forward to it like a kid at Christmas with a gift under the tree, knowing he's getting a wonderful gift, but slightly anxious at not being sure exactly what it is. In some ways, I guess that's what the afterlife is for believers – a wonderful gift, but no way to know how wonderful it is till you get it and experience it. Not that I'm buying all that at this point in my life.

Thursday seemed to pass too quickly, and right after dinner, as we were all settling into the family room, I noticed that a couple of sets of car lights flashed up on and across the wall of the living room, indicating somebody had pulled into the long drive. The lights disappeared off the wall, indicating whoever had arrived would be at the front door before long. No one else in the family room seemed to notice what I'd seen as they were all just having a good time, continuing to reminisce about the past. I departed the group without saying anything. No need to draw attention to myself or our new guests.

When I opened the front door to the house, I slowly made my way across the porch and down the couple of steps to the sidewalk. It was then that I noticed the automatic floodlights with censors from above the garage had lit the driveway to a point I could not only hear but could see our new arrivals. The doors to two cars with what appeared to be out-of-state plates opened, and people began to pour out of the vehicles. It instantly put me in the mind of a circus act I'd seen as a child at Barnum and Bailey's traveling circus, the act in which a bunch of clowns get out of a tiny car, many more than should have fit into vehicles that were smaller than the new Smart Car. With the number of people getting out of each car, followed by the sighs of relief and exaggerated stretching exercises some were doing, it definitely reminded me of the circus act. When combined with some of the group almost tipping over from loss of balance and the laughter that ensued as some stepped over and onto others, my flashback of a circus clown act seemed right on target. The new group of guests, which consisted of some of my dad's cousins, their spouses, and kids realized they had an extra guest in their midst... me... and instantly reacted as if they hadn't seen me since I was a toddler.

"Boy, you sure grow'd up," said Dad's cousin, Dominic, one of a handful of relatives from Jackson, Mississippi.

"Who is it?" Dom's sister and one of Dad's favorites, Renee, asked. I knew she had night-blindness as well and probably was having trouble seeing me as I stood just outside the spotlight of the garage floodlights.

"It's Jared!" I yelled as I walked into the spotlight for her to be able to see me. Once she was able to see me clearly, she squealed, "No way, in Sam Hill. Is't you, son. Fo' real?"

"For real, Renee, it's me." I didn't get to see our Southern family contingent very often, and it was always a treat when we got together. "It's awesome to see all of you guys. So glad you made it in safe from the long road trip . . . If you guys are ready, we'll head on in. Dad will be so excited to see you guys."

Renee's son, Steven, his wife, Britney, and their year-old son, Caleb, were part of the Bagwell contingent. Dominic, Renee's brother, his wife, Debbie, and his two teenage boys from his first marriage were also with the Southern contingent that had just arrived. As I held the front door open, the group filtered through, and I saw that I'd missed the fact that two of the more subdued members of the group, my dad's Uncle Kenny and Aunt Brenda, were with the group as well. "So good to see you guys," I said as I hugged them both. "Always good to see you. I know Dad will be so glad to see you," I said as tears began to well up in my eyes at the sight of these two special relatives.

I could hear the hoopin' and hollerin' coming from the family room as each member of the group made their way into the room; this was one family that was able to break any form of silence, and this was just one of the things I loved about this family. The scene reminded me of where Dad's colorful nature came from. His roots were the South, where his family was from and where many had lived their entire life. He used to say (not around his Southern relatives) that once he realized it was legal to leave the state line (of Arkansas), he crossed the line and never looked back. This seemed partially true, but he loved the South, the people, the food, and the life that seemed to be associated with it, a simpler life. He often said that if people up north could get the spirit and hospitality of Southerners, if global warming could take the edge off the severe winters up north, and if there could be just a splash of mountains and ocean added to the landscape, no one would want to live anywhere else.

When I was younger, I used to think that Dad's family talked louder around Lindsey and me because of our hearing impairment. I finally realized they were just loud and boisterous in a good way. They were a spirited group and had a way of bringing life to any scene they entered.

This evening would be interesting with Mom's more conservative family mixing it up with Dad's party clan. They didn't mean any disrespect to the St. Louis crowd and would try to encourage them to loosen up over the course of the remainder of the evening, which went strong up until 2:00 a.m., for those who didn't concede and hit the sack early.

The atmospheric change of mood was so eye-opening to me when the Bagwell crew arrived at around 7:30 p.m. As my peripheral vision had been closing in more dramatically over the past months, I really had to work at following the multiple conversations that started to take place. It seemed as though Dad's relatives were unaware of the fact that Dad was dying, which we all knew was not the case. They evidently used humor and laughter as a healing agent as the group commenced to cut up with each other and almost immediately started telling stories on each other from the moment they settled into the comfort of the oversized family room.

The stories they started telling moved quickly to the many each of them had on Dad. One of the Bagwell's would refer cryptically to some occurrence in the past, grinning and looking around at the other Bagwell family members, they'd pause, and the whole group would burst into raucous laughter. Within the first hour, many of them were in tears due to the laughter from story after story already told in rapid fire. I just knew a few of us (myself included) might wet our pants if we didn't get a breather soon, which didn't seem to be letting up any time soon.

"Greg, now tell us again cuz we ain't heard the story in a while 'bout you exposin' yourself on that Amtrak on the way to DC," Dom said, barely able to even get his request out as he snickered to which they all started to bust a gut. I'd heard the story a hundred times at least, but never tired of it. It truly was hilarious, and Dad rarely changed up more than two words in the entire story, always using the same exaggerated motions and intonations in his retelling this tale. It was all true, though, as I was a firsthand witness to this, one of many hilarious stories of events in Dad's life. We had one constant question in our house. "Why does this stuff always happen to you, Dad?"

Dad gladly responded to Dominic's request, and he had his audience, which he always enjoyed. "OK, but I'm only tellin' this one if Renee promises to tell the one about her date with the mailman that she picked up at the gynecologist's office last year."

Renee tried to sound innocent with the group (almost like a rehearsed sitcom scene) and scolded Dad. "Now, Greg, you know that ain't true . . . He wasn't just a mailman, and I was not the one doin' the pickin' up in that OB-GYN office. And you know that's the truth . . . But he shore wuz a cutie." She was broadly grinning and laughing in anticipation of her next question. "Greg, now tell us again . . . Now why'd you get naked on that train?" to which the entire group rolled with laughter, and all waiting for Greg to kick into gear with his storytelling, a real talent of Dad's.

Positioning himself so everyone could see and hear, making sure everyone was engaged in active listening, Dad proceeded to tell the group with as much animation as I'd ever seen.

"Well, as you may remember, we decided to take a family vacation back in '05 to Washington DC taking the Amtrak instead of flying from Chicago. We splurged and did the dining car and sleeping car thing. After dinner, I told Sherri and the kids that I was going down the hall to the common shower area to get a shower and head to our berth to read a book and try to get some shut-eye."

Chuckles already started with the group as they knew what was coming, even though their level of intense listening almost gave the thought they'd never heard this story before. Based on the lack of reaction from Mom's family, I figured most of them hadn't heard the story, or maybe they had, and that was the reason for their lack of reaction. At this point, that didn't matter; I could see in Dad's eyes that his fire for life hadn't gone out yet, and he was having a blast.

"So," Dad continued, "I go down the hall and walk into this huge changing area next to the shower. I disrobed and was ready to jump into the shower and, of all things, the train hits a curve, and I fly out into the hall!" Dad's delivery on this part of the story never changed. He would look around the group and rhythmically deliver these words and with surprise in his voice as if he still could not believe this had actually happened.

At this, the whole group is cracking up, including me. I never tired of Dad's many stories, this one being one of my favorites.

As he stands up and reaches up to grab an imaginary door for effect, Dad adds, "I'm trying to pull the door shut, and some woman down the hall – reading her book – puts her book down to check out the noise." Aunt Brenda must have never heard this as she gasped, slapping both her hands up to her mouth. "You have got to be kiddin' me," she howled. Knowing now he has someone in his midst that hasn't heard the story just eggs Dad on. "I know. I couldn't believe it, but since I was already exposed." Still holding his imaginary door, he waves with his other hand and adds, "I just waved."

"What else could I do?" he asked as if the group had a better answer for him. By this time, Dad is almost in tears retelling the story. "I went back into the room, cracking up the whole time I'm taking my shower. I get out, reach for the towel, and . . ." He paused at this point for added effect and blurts out, "That dad-burned train hits another curve, and I fly out a second time!"

The whole room is losing it by now, and some of the group is even dabbing their eyes with their hands or, for the handful of folks who had them, handkerchiefs.

Dad continued and, by this time, he's so into the story that he's standing up. "So there I am . . . again. The lady down the hall is not *even* lookin' up from her book this time, though." All with questioning looks on their faces, anticipating the punch line, which never changed in words or delivery.

"I told a buddy of mine I suppose she just thought I was a pervert to which he replied," – Dad added in a bland replica of his friend's voice as he cleared it for effect – "'Are you kiddin'? She just wasn't interested.'" The group lost it at this point with uncontrollable laughter. It was like that the rest of the evening, story after story and a ton of laughs. This was so typical with Dad's family. They were a hoot and had a zeal for life that always left me wanting more when we'd depart their company.

Mom's family, although pretty conservative, joined in the fun and laughter but didn't believe they had stories to compete or had conceded the night to the Bagwell's and their type A personalities. It was hard to compete with the dominance of Dad's animated family, who all had stories that could have easily been the basis of a sitcom. Regardless, the Benders became the audience while the Bagwells took center stage that night.

# CHAPTER 8

BY 2:00 A.M., there were just a few of the Bagwells left in the family room, and we all sensed this night was a wrap. There would be a lot more laughs with little serious discussions now that the Bagwell clan had arrived, and we didn't even have all of Dad's family in yet. New stories would be coming with the arrival of other family over the next day or so. I could clearly see that the evening had worn Dad out, though, as he actually was looking frail to me for the first time since we'd found out about the malignant tumor that had wrapped itself around the spine, near the base of his head and neck. I knew he had enjoyed the evening, but it had obviously taken its toll. One good thing with his particular type of tumor, there wasn't much pain involved. I would have thought there would be major headaches and severe pain, but fortunately, that wasn't the case.

While most of the remaining family was retiring to their respective quarters, with Mom's guidance to their rooms for the night, I decided to slip on my jacket and get some fresh air out in the backyard. Just wanting a little time to myself and reflect on the night that I believed would become one of my last memories with Dad, I headed back to the log swing at the back of the lot. Even though the path was lined with Malibu lighting, I'd pretty much memorized the walk, knowing how many steps it was from the deck, across the grassy backyard, over the curved stone path, to the opening to the back 40, as we called it. As I exited the stone path through the woods to the opening to the lake, memories flooded my mind of times gone by that I would treasure and that no one could ever steal away from me.

Dad and I had spent untold hours fishing off the wooden dock, which jutted out in a T, about fifty feet past the opening at the end of the path. The dock had a built-in bench seat on the left part of the T, where Dad and I would sit for hours when I was younger, catching and releasing the bass, catfish, and bluegill. We stocked the pond every year, and some of the fish had grown to a pretty good size by now. Dad even caught a fifteen-pound cat (fish) earlier in the summer, which he proudly paraded around the house to show all of us. Mom was ready to kill him when he brought his haul into the kitchen, dripping all over her clean floor. She got over it quickly, though, as she knew the memory of him with the big catch would be something she'd cherish in the years to come, Dad beaming from ear to ear, oblivious to the mess he was leaving behind. For the neat freak he was, when it came to fishing, he was uncharacteristically nonchalant about his messes.

Even though I really didn't like fishing, I loved being with my dad, even when he had seemed so distant and in a world all his own during his substance-abuse days. I never knew how many of those times we spent fishing that he had been drunk or high, but his spirits were always high when we were fishing, so it never mattered to me if he was high on life or something else during those times. He was trying to survive life in the only way he knew back then, but fishing was the one time when he was riding high, regardless. I truly was thankful to God that Dad finally found that Christ was sufficient for him. No longer did he have to work so hard at killing all his senses and emotions to make it through the day.

After stopping at the end of the path, I just stared at what I could make out of the dock, with the past washing over me like a comfortable blanket. All of a sudden, arms reached around and pulled me in close into a bear hug. It didn't startle me but instead gave me a sense that everything in the world was OK even though it seemed that it should be shattering and falling apart. Those once strong arms were so used to wrapping around their son, and as I just soaked in the moment, Dad said in that reassuring deep voice, "I love you more," which had become our little thing. With my sister, the line was "I love you more than you'll ever know."

With my voice breaking ever so slightly with emotion and tears forming in the corner of my eyes, I struggled to get out, "No, I love you more." Once the words released, so did the emotion. I turned around and pulled Dad in even closer, hugging him for all it was worth, wishing this moment would last forever. "Dad, I am going to miss you more than you could possibly imagine," I managed to eek out, barely audible as I sunk my face into Dad's shoulder as I had done so many times as a child with Mom when in need of consoling. This was territory that Dad and I had only found within the past couple of years.

Still hugging him tightly, he simply stated, "Jared, you have the option for this to be the shortest time we spend together and join me with our Creator to infinity and beyond," emphasizing the latter in an imitation of Buzz Lightyear from *Toy Story*. He added after a short pause, "And you know what I mean."

I knew truth but just couldn't seem to make this type of commitment, especially when I still had so many years to live in this world. But knowing how special this moment was for Dad as well as myself, I told him, "I know, Dad . . . In due time, Dad . . . In due time."

As I eased out of our bear hug, arms dropping to my side, I gazed upward into the clear night sky. I couldn't see well enough with my limited peripheral vision to see that Dad was just staring at me.

"Bud, what do you see?" I knew he meant what *could* I see.

"Mostly blackness with a few spots of light, probably about five or so stars," I replied.

"How are you really doing with the RP?" he asked. We had just learned about a year ago after a routine eye exam that I had retinitis pigmentosa, a genetic progressive degeneration of the retina. Combined with my hearing impairment, the progressive sight loss added to my life's challenges, with this most recent diagnosis. When a person had more than one interrelated disease, it was called a syndrome, just one more label to be added to me. In my case, Usher syndrome II was my added label, given my particular type of genetic hearing and eye issues.

The initial symptom was night-blindness, which I had convinced myself wasn't real or just a natural progression of sight for everyone. But when I started to realize that the stars were disappearing from my sight at night and that my peripheral vision was beginning to close in, I had become a little concerned. I really didn't want to believe there was an issue and wrote it off to a need for glasses. But when glasses corrected my farsighted issues but didn't do a thing for my night-blindness, I really became alarmed.

The prognosis from the retinal specialist who delivered the blow to us just twelve short months ago was not promising. He told Mom, Dad, and me who were all there that dreaded day that RP eventually would most likely lead to blindness, and there were no proven treatments or cures. No hope. That's the clearest message I heard that day, but I wouldn't allow myself to completely go there, at least not yet.

I was convinced that with my many years ahead and the progress made on hearing aids in my short life, which I'd worn since I was three, that a cure or treatment would be around the corner and I wouldn't lose my sight. Reality was that deterioration was occurring, slowly but surely, and my hopes were moving quickly to fears for the future. I couldn't imagine not being able to see in addition to having severe hearing loss . . . A loving God wouldn't allow that to happen, right? I figured He was either punishing me or really didn't care about me. Either way, it angered me at God any time I gave it more than a moment's thought.

"Dad," I finally responded as I turned to face Dad, who I could partially make out in the pitch-black night, "I'm fine for now. It's not like I can do anything about it anyway, and quite frankly . . . I'm not gonna let it ruin my life."

I thought I saw a smirk on Dad's face as he raised his hand with a finger raised upward. As if he could read my mind, he said, "Bud, God does love you, and as it says in Psalm 139, you were fearfully and wonderfully crafted in your mother's womb." He added what I was really struggling with these days. "I know it sounds cliché when someone says God won't put you through more than you can handle, but let me tell you something I hope you'll take to heart.

"We absolutely cannot try to understand why God allows things to occur in our lives. We've been through a lot and will be through even more in the days ahead. I know that this doesn't seem fair and sure point to an unloving God by the world's standards. James 1 even states that we will face trials, not leaving any doubt that life has struggles that we all face."

I just shook my head in agreement, following him so far.

"But Jared, I'm here to tell you that one day, it will all make sense, and we'll look back on the shorter part of our lives, our lives here on earth, and we won't have any questions." Pausing, he continued, "Come, join me in about eighty more years, and let's continue this journey together."

"Your mother and I continue to pray for a miraculous healing, son, but I don't know if you know this part and I'm sharing it with you now because of my undying love (no pun intended)." To which I finally released a chuckle. "Know that we have been praying, first and foremost, for your spiritual healing and then for your physical healing for God to open your spiritual eyesight and then heal your physical eyesight."

Giving him a questioning look, I saw the tears now shining off his cheeks as they poured down his face. It was then that he said one last thing that pierced my spirit and soul. "Bud, I'd rather you enter heaven blind than to have you experience hell with twenty-twenty vision. I hope you know that I'm saying that not to be insensitive or mean but because of the love that we and Christ have for you."

I was able to clear my throat and took his face in my hands as I finished this special time together. "Dad, I do know . . ." I choked up, then added, "Both . . . and by the way, I really do love you more." We both released half laughs and half sobs as we ended this special moment by the lake, a memory that I knew I would never forget the rest of my days. One thing I never questioned was my Father's love for me.

Dad was hoping to have some one-on-one time with me soon, and the time out by the lake at the bench on the dock had more than exceeded his desire and expectations. He'd prayed that God would speak through him to me on his way down the narrow path that led to the lake that night; he believed God had done just that, providing him just the right words to say. Upon arriving back at the house, Dad retired into the sunroom, just off the kitchen. The sunroom had become his studio for painting and other creative projects – a room that was completely surrounded on two sides by floor to ceiling windows and an amazing view of the natural surroundings of thick woods and a glimpse of the lake, visible just beyond the end of the stone path.

Sleep wasn't a high priority for Dad these days as he knew his time was limited. So he found himself spending at least a few hours every day after everyone else had gone to bed, working on his secret project, one he hoped and prayed would make an impact for Christ, even if with just one lost or wandering soul.

As he settled into an oversized rattan chair in the sunroom, he reflected on the day that he and Mom had taken me to the retinal specialist to determine whether the ophthalmologist was right in his preliminary diagnosis of their only son – that I had retinitis pigmentosa. That week had been rough before we even got to the appointment with the specialist that we were referred to by the eye doctor. I absolutely lost it the night that we received the preliminary news. I screamed out to Mom and Dad about the unfairness of now having to deal with going blind on top of being hearing impaired. In response to my rage, Dad screamed out in hopelessness with me at the same unfairness. He reached out, grabbed me in a tight hold as we both sobbed uncontrollably.

"Let go of me!" I screamed at Dad as I worked free of his hold. I was so angry at the moment – I couldn't accept anyone's comfort, Dad's or anyone else's for that matter. I thought I would explode from my rage of anger, and as Dad began to tighten his hold on me, I repeated with force, "Let go of me!" With tears forming in his eyes, Dad continued to tighten his hold on me and said something that I will never forget. He looked me straight in my "now-flawed" eyes and said, "I will *never* let go of you, Bud . . . Do you hear me . . . NEVER!"

The day of the appointment with the specialist the next week was surreal and a day that the Bagwell clan wished (or attempted to pray) away. As Dr. Lee, the retinal specialist, and his assistant went through the battery of tests, each one provided further indication that there was an issue. Mom and Dad didn't say a word during the tests, but they sensed with the results of each new test completed that the case was building to confirm the retinal specialist's suspicion that their only son had this degenerative retinal disease that would rob me of my sight eventually.

The first test had been a routine eye chart exam, which was recognizable by all as the standard eye exam – the infamous wall chart with the larger font letters and numbers on the top line, with the font decreasing in size with each descending line of random letters and numerals. The results of this test seemed encouraging as I was seeing more lines than either of my parents were able to see from their vantage point in the room. What none of us realized at the time was the fact that central vision can be perfect with those who are first diagnosed with retinitis pigmentosa. When the peripheral vision test was being completed, however, we had our first inkling that something most likely was not right.

"Tell me what you see at the corners of the page when you focus at this center spot," the doctor inquired as he pointed to the center of the page on the second test, a simple piece of paper that contained a distinctive grid pattern.

"Well, the corners are not real clear. They're actually kinda rounded off and fuzzy." I wanted to lie, but I knew I needed to reply honestly, or I'd just be postponing the inevitable diagnosis of some sort of sight issue that I feared we were about to receive.

The next test required a simple following of Dr. Lee's fingers out to the sides of my head as I looked straight ahead, using only my peripheral vision. It was apparent to Mom and Dad that my peripheral vision was limited (based on my responses) as they both were discretely completing the test themselves as it was being administered to me. Unbeknownst to me, they were both holding their own fingers or hands in similar position to their own heads, mirroring Dr. Lee's distance to my periphery, to complete their own nonscientific determination of whether I was passing this particular test. I was not. In fact, if their unscientific grading of the test was right, I was definitely not seeing everything that I should be able to, especially low or high and outside.

Dr. Lee administered another test for peripheral vision that would prove less subjective. This one gave my parents a needed emotional break and took a full half hour. Essentially, I was escorted into a dark room and led to a small machine. I was told to rest my head against a headrest on the machine and push a handheld button each time I saw a dot appear on the screen while looking straight ahead. At first, I was seeing nothing and figured the machine was malfunctioning, so I started looking up and sideways to ensure the machine was working. Sure enough, I saw a dot appear on what otherwise was a blank canvas and immediately hit the button. Well, I'm sure that skewed the test results as I know I was not looking straight ahead. After that, I decided the test was working, looked straight ahead and was able to identify several dots, pushing the button each time I saw one. I had a strong suspicion I was missing several, though, but knew I had to be honest in all the tests to really determine if there was indeed an issue.

Next came something I'd only had done a couple of times in my life – dilation of the eyes. After dilating my eyes and waiting the appropriate amount of time, Dr. Lee and his assistant took me into a separate room for live x-rays of the retina, which would give a complete 360 view of the entire eye. Mom and Dad wanted to be present for each battery of tests, and this was the one where Dad was totally convinced there was a problem. On the back of the x-rays of my retinas, there appeared to be many dark irregular spots, which Dad knew were not normal, based on a recent eye exam he'd been through and the resulting pictures of his perfectly healthy eye. By the subdued, matter-of-fact instruction that Dr. Lee was giving to his assistant, Dad knew it wasn't looking good. He walked partially out into the hall, where he overheard a group of people who worked at the center quietly talking, but he heard enough of their conversation to further confirm that I, in fact, did have this blinding hereditary disease.

"I believe this is called Usher syndrome. It's when you have RP but also have hearing impairment," one of them said, trying to be discreet.

"Have you seen any case of this? This is the first one I've seen where it wasn't just RP," another said. "I think your chances of winning the lottery are better than having Usher syndrome." Just what Dad needed to hear as he was already about to lose it.

They were just talking among themselves, and they had no reason to suspect or know that Dad had hypersensitive hearing (go figure) and that he was hearing at least portions of their conversation. Not that they were being unprofessional or hurtful in any way. They all appeared to have genuine concern written all over their faces. Dad heard just enough of their private conversations, though, and with his back to the door of the exam room, tears began welling up as he sensed that horrible feeling of déjà vu. Flashbacks flooded Dad's mind of both times he and Mom found out about both Lindsey and my hearing impairment when each of us was about three years of age. Dad felt as if he might have an anxiety attack right then and there, which he'd never had before, a tightening of his chest and extreme dizziness, followed by a feeling that he could throw up at a moment's notice.

Little did Dad know, but Mom was having similar feelings, but she was praying through every step during the battery of tests being run. She was still holding out hope that God would not allow me, her only son, to have yet another health challenge to be forced to live with. She was praying for God to give her the disease, if someone had to have it. She'd seen for her forty-seven years and would have done anything to take my place so I wouldn't have to endure yet another physical impairment.

Yet God, in His infinite wisdom, allowed me to be the one diagnosed with retinitis pigmentosa that day. Reality would slowly and deeply set in, but hope would build over time. Mom and Dad had hoped and prayed that God would allow them to step in and take this on in my stead, much like Christ had stepped in and died on the cross for their sins; that was not to be the case this cold November day a year ago.

Mom and Dad continued to learn what so many before and many to come would learn: you are most vulnerable with your children. The pain of loss with anything dealing with the health of a child is one of the hardest pains for any parent to go through. In this case, it's the one time in life that a parent can't be the hero and step in to take the hurt away.

Little did Mom and Dad know then (or now, for that matter) that Lindsey would be diagnosed with the same degenerative disease of her retina. She had gone to her eye doctor and gotten a clean report that it didn't appear she had RP or Usher syndrome; however, she and John secretly met with Jared's retinal specialist a few months ago, and he confirmed that she did have Usher syndrome. They were grateful for HIPPA and the fact that their medical records were secure as Lindsey and John decided to keep the news to themselves to spare Dad (and Mom, for that matter) from the pain in his last days. There was nothing at this point that could be done from a treatment standpoint anyway, so they decided to not put him through this added mental anguish. Their strong faith and trust in Christ would see them through this new struggle. Their only concern was wondering if the child Lindsey was holding in her womb might also have the genetic defect – not that it mattered to them as they would have had the child regardless.

They wanted their own children, and even with this newfound knowledge, they had only spoken to each other about the fact that they would trust God with the outcome with this and any other pregnancy. Many people would think the decision to have children foolish, but the retinal specialist had told them that their chances of having a child with Usher syndrome or any other genetic defect were no different. After all, as far as they knew, John's family had no history of this disease. But neither Mom nor Dad knew of any family members on either side of their respective families with the disease either, and little would they have ever believed that they were batting two for two.

# CHAPTER 9

LINDSEY AWOKE FIRST in their home the next morning at around 9:00 a.m. She eased down the hall from their bedroom to their tiny kitchen, where she pushed the button on the automatic brewer for coffee that was set up the night before by her hubby. A compulsive reflex these days, she put her hands over her stomach and looked around the room as if unsure what she was supposed to do next.

"Well, beautiful little girl," she said, addressing her baby as she looked down at her unborn child's current home.

"What shall we make for Aunt Faye and the kids for breakfast?" she asked and waited as if she'd get an oral response from her unborn child.

"You think we should make my house-famous pancakes with bacon and scrambled eggs?" Still waiting for the answer from the baby and as if she got the response she was seeking, she responded with, "Excellent idea . . . Hope they like blueberries 'cause these will be exploding with fresh berries."

Aunt Faye had entered the room during the last exchange of discussion Lindsey was having, and her presence slightly startled

Lindsey once she realized she wasn't alone. "So she likes your blueberry pancakes, huh? That's enough of an endorsement for me to know I'll love them too," Faye said as she walked toward Lindsey, and they embraced in a hug.

"I'm so glad you guys came straight here in the middle of the night." Lindsey had left the door unlocked the night before in anticipation of Aunt Faye's arrival at around 1:00 a.m. and had given her instruction to just come on in and make themselves comfortable. "What time did you guys make it in? No problems finding the place? Did the whole crew come with you or . . . ?" Lindsey finally realized that she was rattling off questions in rapid succession and said, "I'm sorry, here I'm just going on and on and not even giving you time to respond."

Faye just looked at her with an approving, loving look and shook her head with pursed lips. "Lindsey, first off, you look amazing. How far along are you now? Do you know what you're having? Natural or epidural?"

They both had a quiet laugh and then they proceeded to answer each other's questions and added a bunch more to the mix while Lindsey was working on her house-famous Nelson breakfast. She wasn't known for being the best cook but figured she was safe with this, one of her few standard offerings. We'd all convinced her after several food preparation experiments, which she had tortured us with since she said "I do," that this was one she'd perfected . . . well, almost.

John walked in during the exchange of conversation between his bride and Aunt Faye when they were getting up to date on each other's lives. "What's burnin'?" he asked as he scrunched his nose up, sniffing noisily.

"Oh, my gosh," Lindsey responded, almost flying from her seated position at the kitchen table and heading quickly toward the oven, which was already beginning to form clouds of billowing smoke from its top. She opened the oven up slowly, with dish towel in her hand, and started fanning the cloud of smoke that burst forward. The smoke almost completely swallowed Lindsey to the point she could barely be seen but easily found from her instant coughing response. Immediately as if on cue, the smoke alarm went off to which their little shih tzu, Millie, scurried in, barking at the scene and everyone in it. A couple of Faye's kids came running in, yelling, "What's wrong? Is the house on fire?" John proceeded to open the backdoor and pushed open a window to let the smoke filter out of the small room. "No, guys, no house fire, but we really need to get this smoke out of here to prevent that dad-gummed smoke detector from going off again and stop it from chirping anymore."

Almost zombielike, a still-sleepy John got up on a chair under the smoke detector and hit the reset button. It stopped, and on his way down out of the chair, another alarm went off in the direction of the front door. He methodically moved to the foyer smoke detector to repeat the process as if this was a normal occurrence around the Nelson household. In less than a minute, the house became quiet again, well, other than Millie, who continued to bark incessantly as if she was protecting the group from some additional unknown danger. The smell of burnt breakfast quickly filled the little bungalow.

"Well, that was exciting," Faye said as she raised her eyebrows and bit her upper lip as if she didn't need to say more.

"I'm so sorry. I guess I put the oven up too high to keep the bacon warm," Lindsey said, and with that, Aunt Faye let out an airy sigh and visibly relaxed her shoulders, giving added reassurance to Lindsey that everything was fine. As Lindsey gingerly pulled out some bacon that was burnt to a crisp, Faye added, "I'm sure they'll be just fine. We actually like our bacon 'well-done.'" Lindsey just mouthed 'I'm sorry" to her aunt and shrugged her shoulders with her arms outstretched and palms raised as if further emphasizing 'Oh well.'

By this time, John had already grabbed a handful of charred bacon and had crunched into it. Talking with his mouth full, he said, "Tastes fine . . . Kind of like . . . like a . . . burnt bacon."

Lindsey, still with her dish towel in hand, immediately responded without time for thought. She twirled the dish towel tight and snapped it at John, based on his smart-alecky comment. It popped loudly, hitting its mark perfectly, making an immediate red mark on John's bare leg, just below the hem of his pajama shorts.

"That's gonna cost ya," John delivered with deadpan seriousness to Lindsey, just smiling as if his scheme was already being formulated in his mind to get her back when she least expected it.

"Boys, let's help set the table," Aunt Faye politely said to her boys. "Sure don't want our breakfast to get cold . . ."

"Yeah, cold and burnt is not a pretty combo," John said as he grinned from ear to ear at Lindsey, who just made a face of disappointment but knowing everything would be fine.

# CHAPTER 10

**M**OM TYPICALLY HAD to awaken at a slow pace in the mornings, going through a new routine process of staring at Dad for a while and then turning toward the window in wonderment as to what kind of day she was about to encounter. She enjoyed all sorts of days, whether sunny, stormy, hot and humid summer day, or bitter cold with whiteout snowstorms; she loved the seasonal extremes of Northern Illinois. Dad, on the other hand, said anyone who stated that they enjoyed the bitter winters in Chicagoland, when nostrils froze when you inhaled and thawed when you exhaled, needed their head examined. As Mom was going through the first part of her morning ritual, staring at her hubby of twenty-five years, she noticed that he looked a little too peaceful and still on this particular morning. Psalm 46:10 came to her mind at that moment, and she knew it was God speaking to her. "Be still and know that I am God." God's Word, which normally comforted Mom, didn't have the same effect this specific morning, however, as Dad's stillness didn't seem quite right.

She snuggled into Dad, hoping and praying with all her might that he was still with her, to which he almost seemed to respond with a raise of his arms above his head, stretching and yawning, then embracing his bride of twenty-five years, his soul mate, the love of his life. She sighed with relief. She allowed God's Word spoken just moments earlier to wash over her – this time in comfort.

"I love you so much." Dad knew this was the best greeting he could give to Mom each and every morning. Many mornings, he'd quietly slip out of bed, walk gingerly to her side of the bed, tell her that he loved her in his quiet voice, gently kiss her on the cheek so he wouldn't awaken her, and head off to start his day. Rarely did he miss the opportunity to kiss her and tell her that he loved her each morning before he left her sound asleep in their bedroom, but he evidently missed at least once as I recall Mom laying into him one time for not telling her he loved her before leaving their bedroom. He was taken aback by the comment since he was always careful to not wake her up. Mom told him that it always woke her up, but she would normally drift back to sleep, with the knowledge that her husband loved her for yet another day. They both knew love was a choice and not a feeling. It was much like their faith; they had decided over the past few years, something that shouldn't be based on feelings and knowing there would ultimately be a wonderful outcome based on their choice, both in love and in faith.

"And I . . . love you, too," Sherri responded. "We have a big day ahead of us but can't we just stay here all day, right? It's great to have family and friends in but can't we just be selfish and spend the day right here, just the two of us?"

"Why not? We should be able to just stay here in each other's arms until He's ready for me," Dad said as if that really was a valid choice. After thinking about the possibilities for a split second, he raised his eyebrows and reached over to the nightstand for the remote control for the TV, which they rarely ever watched in the bedroom. It was purposed more for the wonderful soft jazz music that had become a standard for this couple's listening pleasure. Mom knew there was only one reason Dad would turn on jazz this early in the morning, and she had read his intentions correctly.

"Let me quote the Song of Solomon this morning, my dear," Dad said this as he gently pushed Mom's hair off of her face, cupping her face in his hands, as Mom just closed her eyes to enjoy this time. "Your lips drop sweetness as the honeycomb, my bride. Milk and honey are under your tongue," Dad quoted while he was stroking her face gently, drawing on her face (as she called it) with a light touch that sent chills up and down her spine. Mom opened her eyes as she knew she wanted to remember this time for years to come. They embraced closer and spent the next hour enjoying what God had so wonderfully created, intimacy that was designed for a man and a woman, a time when two truly became one.

When I got up, it seemed odd that the usual smells weren't wafting up the stairs, making their way under my door and to my hypersensitive nostrils. I decided maybe my allergies had kicked in, and my smeller just wasn't working right 'cause I was sure Mom would already be up and about. I bounded down the stairs two steps at a time and found Grandpa Bender reading a small leather-bound book that I assumed was a Bible. It was apparent that he'd figured out how to make a pot of coffee as he was sipping the warm brew as I walked into the family room.

"Hi, Pops, see ya found the coffee."

"Yeah, already made. All I had to do was hit the button," he said, still flipping through some of the thin pages of his book as he glanced over the top of his glasses at me. It put me in the mind of Dad as I peered into the cozy surroundings of our family room, coffee mug in hand with the steam rising up toward his glasses, head tilted in pensive thought at what I now knew were the scriptures. Just like Dad on any given day, he was reclined in one of the oversized burgundy leather chairs in the family room, floor light turned on low, to enhance the natural morning light that was angling throughout the room in beams that made it appear that God had even put a subdued spotlight on Grandpa B.

"You need something, Bud?" Grandpa asked as he pulled his glasses off, twirling them with one hand by one arm of the glasses, another image that put me in the mind of Dad since he did the same thing when taking a break from reading to talk to me.

"No, Gramps. I'm fine. Don't need a thing, but I am wondering what's keeping Mom this morning."

"I think I'd let that sleeping dog lie this morning," Grandpa stated matter-of-factly as he looked at me over the top of his glasses he'd put back on. Without another word, he then focused his attention back to his Good Book, hoping I got the message.

"Huh?" I questioned.

"Never mind, Bud, I'm sure she and your dad will be down soon."

"OK." Then it dawned on me what he was alluding to, and I let out a silent duh to myself, actually happy that my parents could still enjoy each other even in the midst of adversity.

About that time, Mom came floating into the kitchen, humming a jazzy tune. Come to think about it, she hummed a lot of jazz tunes these days, especially on Sundays after church, must have been an XM station on satellite or some Jazz Sundays radio station. I rolled my eye at myself as I pieced the music to the . . . Well, let's just say . . . Actually, let's just not say . . . I just snickered when I saw Mom and tried my best to act nonchalant but knowing more than she thought I knew, based on Pop's subtle tip-off.

"How is everyone this beautiful Friday morning, Budster?" Mom inquired as she refocused her energies on the morning's breakfast preparation.

"We're just peachy keen, Mrs. Clever," I said. "How's 'Ward'?"

She ignored my question, proceeded to the refrigerator, and started pulling out all kinds of raw ingredients for what appeared to be an omelet station in its infancy. It ended up being one of those gigantic egg casserole dishes with sausage, cheese, and bacon, accompanied by waffles. Dad made his entrance as Mom was arranging the ingredients for her egg casserole, and he began assisting Mom with the breakfast as did Grandma and Aunt Cindy, who had also just made their way into the kitchen. Good thing there was plenty of room in Mom's newly renovated Tuscany-styled kitchen as it was beginning to get rather crowded.

"Good mornin', beautiful," Dad said as he kissed Mom with what they referred to as their trifecta (a peck on the lips, then one on the nose, ending with the last peck on the forehead). It was a traditional triple kiss between the two of them, and if Dad omitted any one of the three, Mom would instantly put on her pouty face and cross her arms in disappointment. The omissions were always intentional to get a rise out of Mom, followed by Dad kissing the omitted area, obviously pulling off the tease. So predictable and so wonderful at the same time to have their special intimate moment that could be shared regardless of whether or not they had an audience. No one would have made issue of this display of affection as it seemed rather innocent for a married couple to make everyone around know without a doubt that there was a deep love between the two.

"Mornin', good lookin'," Mom responded. It was everything in me to say, "Cut the act, you two love doves. Some of us are pretty certain you've been doing more than kissing already this morning," but I was soaking it in. There were so many times during the dark ages, as I internally referred to them, when affection was missing altogether, so it was more than all right to hear and see them showing affection toward one another like this. During those darkest of days, it appeared Mom and Dad were more like roommates that tolerated each other more than a husband and wife who should have been in love. I was grateful for the public display of affection (a.k.a. PDA) with these two these days. I could sense that Grandma and Grandpa Bender were just as pleased with Mom and Dad's outward affection as well. They just grinned in toadlike smiles, covering their upper lips with their lower lips as they watched these two, who couldn't seem to get enough of each other these past few years.

I saw Dad stop and grimace, blinking his eyes as if startled with pain, something he didn't have with this type of tumor. Something didn't seem right. Apparently, Uncle Gail saw Dad's pained look too as he was walking into the room. He looked over at Dad with a look of concern and said, "Greg, you OK?" holding out his arm toward Dad. At Gail's question, everyone had turned their focus toward Dad, wondering what was causing the concern.

"Yeah, just give me a minute," Dad said, closing his eyes tight as he gingerly seated himself on a bar stool in front of the kitchen island.

He seemed OK and more embarrassed than anything at this point by what seemed to be just a fluke.

"Maybe you guys shouldn't have had the ... uh ... extracurricular activity this morning," I had directed my comment toward Mom to which half the room busted up laughing, including Mom, and to a lesser degree, Dad. Uncle Gail actually spit what appeared to be a piece of fruit that he'd just put in his mouth, projectiling it across the room with a gut-wrenching laugh. The shot of humor did seem to ease Dad's discomfort and embarrassment as he just shook his head, pointing at me. "Bud, I sometimes forget you're an adult, but a comment like that ... It makes it really hard for me to call you kid."

"Yeah, like I didn't know what was going on when I was a kid?" My emphasis on "kid" caused a reaction in Mom.

"You're incorrigible," Mom scolded as she almost threw the words at me. Always the sensitive one, she reversed her comment as if someone might believe she might really be upset with me. "Oh, I didn't mean that, Bud. You just caught me off guard. You know that I love you."

Mom had a great sense of humor but was pretty guarded and reserved with people she didn't know. However, once she was comfortable with someone, we never knew what would come out of her mouth, shocking most the first time she did it, given her demure image. We would tell people who were just getting to know prim-and-proper Mom that she was actually pretty sarcastic to which she always took an immediate and defensive position. She was so predictable, and we knew the accusation of her sarcastic nature would get a rise out of her, and it was worth watching her spend the next several minutes trying to convince everyone that she was not sarcastic.

"I am not sarcastic," she'd say. "The definition of sarcasm is when someone makes fun of something or someone with malicious intent toward the individual."

Someone in the family would usually add, "So is that *Webster's* definition or your version? We can go find the dictionary, but bet your picture is next to the word." She challenged me on this one time as I was egging her on big-time, so I went into the study, grabbed *Webster's*, and proudly brought it back into the room. She opened it up to the word, and lo and behold, there was a picture of her taped next to the word "sarcastic." As everyone in the room was watching her every move for the word search in *Webster's*, our family just rolled on the floor laughing when her picture was literally next to the word "sarcastic." Mom seemed shocked at first that she was found anywhere in *Webster's* and then she busted up in roaring laughter. Being the proverbial prankster, she just pointed to the guilty party who'd "planted" the picture, and that guilty party was me. "You . . ." was all she could get out, but it spoke volumes in her accusation, trial, and conviction of me, and rightfully so.

There was typically a lot of laughter in our home, and these days it was with each other and not done at someone else's expense as it had been in days past. When you grow up in an alcoholic's home, you expect a degree of drama and chaos. What we were now experiencing was joy and peace. I decided that I could get used to this, as unnatural as it seemed at times. Mom continued to drill it into our heads that we (the entire family) were all on the same team. She'd try to use sports analogies, but with her lack of knowledge of sports, they never seemed to hit the mark. Still the analogies were hilarious and provided for additional entertainment for all of us.

# CHAPTER 11

THE NELSONS FINISHED their breakfast without additional drama since Lindsey's overdone breakfast incident. Millie had even calmed down but still was following any human movement in the house. Typically, if someone got up and moved, she'd get up and follow the person till they petted her, gave her a treat, or threw a chew toy. If they ever did the latter, they were committed for at least the next five to ten minutes of their life to her. Everyone was finishing with showering and getting ready, which took a bit of time, based on the fact that John and Lindsey only had one spare bathroom. They were thankful to have a spare bathroom at all, given the fact that their house of two had grown overnight to a house of seven. Lindsey had always admired her aunt Faye's strength and determination while maintaining a sense of femininity, making her one of her favorite aunts. She was thrilled to have her as a guest in her home, playing the role of hostess for the first time. Aunt Faye's husband had left her for reasons that were not quite known about five years ago, leaving her with four children to raise – all boys.

A strong, independent woman, Faye still seemed fragile at times, but now that her two oldest boys were in their upper teens, they made sure no one ever again harmed their mother. They were very protective of the lone female of their immediate family, a woman who not only was the dominant parental figure, but the sole provider and protector of the boys. The kids had limited interaction with her ex, but she encouraged them to spend time with him, never disparaging him, as best anyone around her could tell. He had since remarried, which most believed to be the source of their marital issues, a lady fifteen years his junior, who was a receptionist at his accounting practice. The emotional scars he had left with the family ran deep, but the five of them had not just survived the past five years but came out of the destruction of their family as a very strong unit. Faye had a strong faith, which she would always cite as the source of her strength and something she delighted in passing on to her boys.

They were just about done with their breakfast when the phone rang.

John picked it up. "Hey, wuz up?" Aunt Faye wasn't sure if this was an atypical Chicago greeting or if the caller ID on his cell phone had given him the identity of the caller, who was someone he knew and was comfortable with such a greeting. She hoped the latter, but he had such a laid-back, relaxed demeanor about him; she wasn't sure, and it really didn't matter anyway.

"How long ago?" John asked, seeming to switch personalities, becoming Mr. Serious all of a sudden. He also had become less animated as he asked, "Which hospital?"

"We're on our way," followed by the sound of broken glass in the next room.

Lindsey had overheard the conversation and filled in the blanks for herself. She had lost her grip, literally and figuratively, dropping a glass of water on the tile floor in their bathroom, which shattered upon impact, leaving a watery and dangerous broken glass mess, which was found in every direction of her bare feet.

"John?" was all she could get out as tears began forming in her eyes, ready to pour out at any second. She slipped her hands beneath their unborn child as if to protect it from what she feared most these days – bad news about her dad.

"It is Dad, and it doesn't sound good," John said as he searched Lindsey's eyes, hoping to protect her with his own calmness in the situation. "Do not move, Lindsey . . . There's glass everywhere, and I'm coming in to get you." Lindsey remained frozen and expressionless until John walked into the bathroom to get her away from the broken shards of glass that surrounded her. Once he made his way to her, she collapsed into his arms. For the first time since they'd been married, John had referred to our father as Dad. "We need to hurry over to St. Luke's . . . Should be able to get there in ten minutes max." He peered into Lindsey's eyes and, with a reassuring and gentle stroke of her face with one hand, spoke to her in as calm a voice as he could muster. "Lindsey, are you OK? We're all here for you. I'm right here and won't leave your side . . . you understand?"

"I'm fine," she said as she tried to remain composed as best she could under the circumstances, already placing her shoes on her feet. "Can we do one thing quickly before we head out . . . please?" She looked around the room at the entire group of six family members, which by now had all congregated into the family room, as she made her request.

"Whatever you want, Lindsey," Faye said. "You name it."

Without delay, Lindsey pleaded in a teary voice, "We've got to pray, then we leave."

John grabbed her hand and one of the younger nephew's hands, leading the group to form a circle. Once they all had joined hands, John led them in prayer. "Dear Lord, we don't want to waste time here." Realizing this sounded wrong, he continued, "It's never a waste of time when we're talking to you, Lord. You know the situation with Lindsey's dad, and we ask that you'd be with him right now. We ask for your will to be done, and selfishly, we ask for you to help him make it through this day. You are our sovereign God, and we trust you completely. Amen." At the close to the prayer, the group silently and solemnly walked toward and out the door.

The dog had sensed that something wasn't right. Millie had walked up to Lindsey and was whimpering as she lay prone at Lindsey's feet, looking up at her with an expression of concern. This dog seemed to have greater understanding than many adults. Lindsey reached over and patted Millie on the head. "It's going to be all right, Millie . . ." She teared up at that, and they headed out the door.

The ambulance had arrived within ten minutes of the call to 911 that Uncle Gail made after Dad collapsed to the floor when he had attempted to stand up from the stool in the kitchen. Mom dropped on her knees beside him and started to check his vitals to determine if he was conscious and, if so, assess how bad the situation. She looked at him questioningly without saying a word after her check of vitals, which seemed weak, but stable. Dad merely looked up at her with his big brown eyes, which he could barely keep open, and in a weak voice, said, "Have I ever told you that you're the most beautiful wife I've ever had?" At that point, he began drifting in and out of consciousness, head slowly bobbing all the while.

With tears of fear welling up in her eyes, Mom was totally oblivious to the commotion in the house as the remaining family members were filling each other in on what had just happened, all of them worried sick. She leaned in closer to Dad, lifting his head gingerly with her arm wrapped around the back of his neck and whispered, "And you are almost the best looking husband I've ever had." This was another of their silly little exchanges that we'd seen them repeat over and over, but this time, as I stood frozen in fear in the center of the kitchen, I wasn't humored by their exchange. I was absolutely not ready to give my dad up, not here and not now. We all felt helpless, and I got that sinking feeling that he was slipping away from us before our eyes as we waited for what seemed an eternity for the ambulance to arrive.

I vaguely recall the sound of sirens getting louder as the ambulance neared the house, then silence. The doorbell didn't even ring as a stretcher and two paramedics wheeled noisily through the foyer and into the kitchen. One of the cousins had been watching for them and had ushered them in, guiding them to the kitchen, where Dad was still laying prone on the kitchen floor, head still resting in Mom's arms; there was no doubt that he was now fully unconscious. When vitals were taken and the paramedics knew he was relatively stable for the moment, they picked him up gingerly and carefully placed him on the stretcher. We were unsure if they weren't communicating to us because of the severity of the situation or if they were trained to share minimal information with family due to some privacy regulation or fear of lawsuits that seemed out of control in the medical field. Tort law needed to be reformed, but that debate would be saved for another day and another battle.

"Is he gonna be OK?" I asked hesitantly, knowing I really wasn't sure I wanted the answer to my question.

"We're doing everything we can," the large-framed guy said. "I'd suggest you guys meet us at the ER at the new Sherman Hospital on Randall. We should be there within fifteen minutes."

"We'll be right behind you."

Knowing Mom was still in her nightgown, I asked how quickly she could get changed. She was relatively calm by this point, stating it'd take her no more than five minutes. It wasn't even that long. She ran upstairs, changed into a pair of capris and a crop top, pulled her long brunette hair back into a ponytail, and was back downstairs in record time. Her long hair gave her that youthful look. The reality of the length of her hair had more with her goal of donating "locks of love," and she only had another inch or so to go before they'd cut off the majority of her hair for some person in need of a wig. She was continually looking for ways to serve and give back, this just being one more example of her thoughtfulness and selflessness.

"Let's go," she firmly directed me. Shifting her attention toward Grandma and Grandpa Bender, she said, "Mom, Dad, please finish up breakfast for me. Make yourselves at home. We'll call from the hospital and let you know how Greg's doing as soon as we know something."

Grandpa B had already eased out of the leather recliner and walked toward Mom as she was leaving her last-minute instructions. He held out his arms, softly embraced his eldest child, and though he was emotionally choked up, was able to eek out, "Love ya, munchkin."

At this, Mom melted like butter and released the emotion that had been building, bawling uncontrollably as she sunk her head into her dad's chest, "Daddy, I just don't think I can do this."

She stiffened, pulled herself away from her dad, wiped her tears with the side of one of her arms and walked away from him while heading toward the front door. "I can't do this." As tears were flowing, she said it again, only louder. "I can't do this!" She continued repeating "I can't do this" over and over, getting louder each time as she pulled at her hair and shook uncontrollably. Totally out of character for this strong woman that was a pillar of strength in our immediate family.

My heart was breaking for Mom. I knew I'd be OK, but I was getting really concerned about her at this point. She'd been so strong up until this moment, but she was obviously losing it now. I feared that she would literally break into pieces right before my eyes. I'd never seen her so fragile.

Grandpa Bender had caught up with Mom just shy of the front door, took his hand, and very gently lifted Mom's face by her chin so they were facing each other. In a firm, calm, and reassuring voice, he got Mom's attention as her pleading eyes spoke to her daddy with an unspoken "Help me." "Sherri, we are here for you. We're not going anywhere. God will give us all the strength we need to get through this, OK?" Mom closed her eyes and pursed her lips as tears continued to stream down her face. She pulled herself into Grandpa and simply replied, "I know, Dad. I really do know. Thanks. I need you here right now and am so glad you're here."

At this, Grandma had walked over as well as Dad's cousins, Mom's brothers, and other family members. Grandpa had been the patriarch of the Bender family for quite some time, and as the spiritual leader of their family, he simply let the group know that prayer was in order. He instinctively prayed for Dad, peace for the family, and for God's strength, power, and wisdom during this difficult time.

Mom seemed to have calmed down just being in the presence of Grandpa's calm and reassuring resolve. Once Grandpa B had completed the prayer, Mom grabbed my hand firmly, let out a long-winded sigh, and led me toward the garage door.

"Let's go, Bud. Your dad needs us."

The rest of the day was a blur for the family as we waited at Sherman Hospital, about fifteen minutes away from the house. The waiting room was taken over by our family as more of them had arrived at the ER and directed to join the rest of the family in the room not intended for this big a crowd. We'd move from an intently serious group to lightheartedness, which helped minimize the intensity of the day. While laughter would break out with a group of the clan, a number of others were in deep thought, staring out into space, lost in their thoughts. This went on for hours, and every time the door opened to the waiting room, our collective heads would turn toward the door. Deafening silence, as if on cue, would filter throughout the room every time that door opened. It became a day that seemed would never end. At around 10:00 p.m., a doctor came in and asked my Mom, Lindsey, John, and I to follow him out into the hallway. At this, my anxiety finally surfaced as I feared what he was about to tell us – that Dad was gone. I thought I'd prepared myself for those fateful words, but at that instant, I knew that I was not ready to give him up. He had become my rock, my role model, and was now the father I'd longed for my entire life. I hadn't had enough time with this transformed man and at that moment prayed to God that we just have another day with him, just one more day. That was to be the last time we spoke to the doctor that day.

# CHAPTER 12

OTHER FRIENDS AND family had made it into town throughout the day and into the chilly November night in Northern Illinois that Friday, the day before the scheduled funeral service. Dad had made arrangements for everyone and had actually booked a block of rooms for everyone who had committed to be there at a brand-new chain hotel that had just been completed within the past year. It was one of those moderately priced, no-frills hotels that had a decent continental breakfast in the morning but no pool or restaurant. Dad's cousin, Dominic, had taken the post at the lake house in case out-of-towners arrived there or called, so they knew what had happened. He also had Dad's cellular phone so he could intercept those calls and provide the news about Dad.

Dom knew somebody needed to fill this role, and he didn't mind. Mom's brother, Rob, and his wife, Angie, took the post at the hotel, making sure no one had to hear about the events of the day any other way than face-to-face with a caring relative. Aunts, uncles, cousins, and a large number of Mom and Dad's friends for life, as they called them, all made it in without incident and getting what rest they could, given the circumstances and the new news. Both Dom and Rob had a list of friends, who they proactively called during the lull times to update each of them on what had happened this day as well, to prepare them for the funeral service, which now would not include my dad as a guest. For something that seemed so odd to me in the beginning, now took an odd twist. It actually seemed odd to me now that Dad wouldn't be there.

My dad's uncle RT and aunt Jane were two of the last of the out-of-towners to arrive at the lake house around 1:30 a.m. Most of the family had returned to the house by that time, and when we answered the knock on the door from RT and Jane, they instantly knew something was wrong, without a word being spoken. Once he had gotten the details from Renee, he asked to speak with Mom, who had headed upstairs to her bedroom just thirty minutes ago. Renee knew that Mom would want to talk to RT, given the close relationship she and Dad had with this uncle. RT slowly made his way up to Mom's bedroom where they had a private conversation for thirty minutes or so. He rejoined Jane downstairs, and they retreated to one of the spare bedrooms that they'd been assigned to for their stay. I had never seen Uncle RT so quiet and serious, unusual for this laid-back man who was typically a spark of life to any party. He looked absolutely spent.

Dad was always careful as to not play favorites with his kids, his cousins, as well as other family, but there was one special uncle, who'd become like a surrogate father to him when his father had passed away when Dad was merely thirteen years of age. RT was his dad's only full-blood brother. Their mother had died of tuberculosis when Grandpa Bagwell was around eleven, and Great-uncle RT was about four years of age. I always believed that Dad's uncle RT knew firsthand what it was like to not have a parent during those difficult and awkward teenage years. RT wanted to be there not only for Dad but to step in and fill a need for his deceased brother too.

RT and his wife, Jane, had never had children of their own, but they had hearts the size of the state in which they'd retired, Texas. Living in Galveston near the coast, the mid-70s couple didn't get the chance to visit family as much as they were able to when he and his wife lived in St. Louis. But that didn't stop him and Dad from talking regularly. Phones still worked between Illinois and Texas, and Dad and RT had an unwritten pact to talk at least every week to two. Dad was always filling me in on their conversations and the endless stories about their family history that Dad would learn from RT, who'd become the Bagwell patriarch, the elder statesman of the family.

Dad revered his Uncle RT, and just like with any close family member, they had their moments of disagreement as well. But one thing was certain; the bond and love between these two was unshakable. The older I became, the more alike, I realized, the two of them were, provided you took away the dissimilarity of addiction and the full head of hair RT had. Dad must have inherited his mother's genes with his bald top, which he chose to shave, a good look for him, certainly in style, and he was able to pull it off better than most.

Neither of them cared for sports but loved being with family when major sporting events like a World Series or Super Bowl were aired. Although they both adopted their own city's sports teams to support, they shared the common thread of support for the St. Louis teams: Cardinals and Rams. Our entire family had become Cubs fans and Bears fans, but if I hadn't been so into sports, Dad's interest level would have been much less in either team. I knew he got into the games to spend time with me more than a genuine interest in the NFL or MLB.

Both Dad and RT had artistic bents to them – Dad with his landscape oil paintings, and RT more proficient in pen-and-ink drawings of people. Some of RT's were a tad risque and were only shared with certain people who could appreciate the "body in art form," as he would say. He was reluctant to show them to most, but he shared them many years ago with me when I was around ten years old. I thought they were awesome and extremely realistic, wishing I had such a talent and feeling like I'd seen something I probably shouldn't be looking at – almost pornographic. It appeared to me that the artistic talent seemed to skip every third generation, based on the fact that both RT and Dad had a gift of artistry, and no one in my generation was able to paint anything other than a house exterior at best.

Both Dad and my great-uncle RT were extremely animated and were great storytellers too. When the two of them were together with the family during the holidays, we were sure to be entertained with their unbelievable knack of telling stories. Laughter abounded, and we knew that stories told by either had been embellished to some degree, but no one cared. The rest of the Bagwell clan were entertaining in their own right, and you felt like you were at a three-ring circus when the entire family was together, never a dull moment and sure to have a good time. I learned to laugh with Dad's family and learned intellectual stimulation and seriousness from Mom's family, a good balance for living and like night and day when with each family unit.

RT and Dad discovered another similarity between the two of them recently. They had both gotten involved in drama at their respective churches and hadn't even known the other was involved in this ministry until recently. With both of them being so dramatic to begin with, this seemed a natural extension of their personas that could be shared with and enjoyed by others. I actually was the one that got Dad involved in drama. In my early teenage years, I asked him to go try out with me for a part in a medieval skit at church, which required British accents. Dad said he'd take me to try out as he'd done in the past. I corrected him, telling him again that I wanted him to try out with me. With his animated nature and dramatic storytelling, I figured he'd be a natural. He looked at me like I had three heads but reluctantly agreed to go along for the ride.

One thing I knew for certain going into the tryouts was he could mock all kinds of accents and figured this would be to his advantage in securing a part. Given that one of his coworkers was from the United Kingdom, all he had to do was talk as if he was David, his coworker friend. He nailed the tryout, got a main part, and his "acting" career in church skits and plays began. Interestingly enough, I'd gotten a part in every church and school drama I'd ever tried out for, and I didn't secure a part this particular time. At least, I got to enjoy watching Dad as he made his debut.

He got hooked on drama after this, and one could tell he was having a blast and quite a natural talent on stage. The very next church drama involved just a husband and wife going through their various "scripts" of life, and they called him, requesting he try out for the skit, which he secured with his first reading. He became a regular, appearing on stage with almost every drama at church from that point forward.

People couldn't believe it when I told them he had no training and did his first gig after turning forty. It got to be pretty humorous as Dad became known around our one thousand five hundred – person congregation as the drama guy. In fact, he and Mom were at a church wide dinner one night, and somebody walked up to Dad, asking where his wife was, looking directly over Mom's head as they searched for Dad's wife. They were serious too. Mom, sitting right beside him, realized that the guy was talking about Mary Ann, who had become his stage wife in many of the skits. Mom simply said, "Oh, I think you're talking about his stage wife. I'm actually the one that does his laundry," to which Dad burst out into laughter. This was just another confirmation of Mom's sarcastic nature, but she still wouldn't concede to that fact.

RT and Dad had a tight relationship, and even though Dad had six other wonderful aunts and uncles with which he had great relationships with, RT was the one to whom he was closest. Dad was always careful not to use the "favorite" descriptive because he didn't want to hurt any of the rest of the group. He loved them all and would never do anything to hurt any of them, but it didn't take a rocket scientist to determine that Dad was closer to RT than the rest of the aunts and uncles. Oh well, that was Dad – always concerned about others, sometimes to a fault.

# CHAPTER 13

SATURDAY MORNING. THE time had come, and Dad's absence would be felt by all this entire day. It was time for the funeral service at the movie theater in neighboring Elgin, Illinois. I had previously called the service a memorial service since it was never intended to have a body in a coffin there, which was what we were accustomed to in traditional family funerals. We hadn't even had anyone on either side cremated in my lifetime, something Dad was about to change.

Friends and family began filtering into the movie theater at around 9:30 a.m., with a steady flow continuing until the large theater was close to two-thirds full, with about two hundred people filling the seats. Once everyone was seated in the theater, which typically was used for IMAX movies, the lights dimmed, and as choreographed, the big screen came to life, right on schedule at 10:00 in the morning.

It was strange, to say the least, to have Dad's face slowly filling up the big screen. He appeared on screen in a familiar setting, behind the lake house, sitting in an oak Adirondack chair, with his back facing the lake behind the house. The setting looked like something off a movie set, with the sunlight bouncing off the still lake behind him, shimmering like glitter. The willows and other trees surrounding the foreground on our side of the lake were crisp and clear while the tree line on the other side wasn't completely in focus for this video clip. All you saw was nature, other than Dad and the chair. Dad so loved the outdoors, and this setting seemed very befitting. It looked like he had this filmed in September as fall colors weren't present in the scene, and Dad seemed comfortable in khaki shorts and a denim shirt with his sleeves partly rolled up.

"Well," Dad began. "First off, I appreciate each of you being here today, and I hope and pray that this service will be more understood as our time today progresses. I've pretaped this message to you for one or two reasons. One, I knew that I wouldn't be able to do this live without my emotions being totally out of whack. Meaning, I'd be bawling like a baby, and you wouldn't be able to understand a word I said. Or two, I am no longer with you."

At this, you could already hear sniffles throughout the audience, but everyone could sense that each person in attendance wanted to soak everything in, so emotions seemed to be controlled as best as could be expected.

"Also, and this is important, I wondered if you would be able to see the hairs up my nose on such a large screen," he said as he leaned in with head cocked upward, pulling his lips downward so we could get a good view. As Dad settled back in the chair on screen, he added, "Ya' know, it just cracks me up that hair stopped growing on top of my head years ago but grew in my nose and ears like I doused both with miracle grow. What is that about anyway? I'm definitely asking God that question when – or if – I'm up there."

A little sparse, almost uncomfortable, laughter came from a spattering of people, many looking around, rolling their eyes, or shrugging at others, in questioning looks toward others as to Dad's intent and use of humor. I snickered and figured this was just the beginning, knowing Dad. I was one of the participants in the snickering crowd, soaking in these last humorous moments I would be able to enjoy Dad's antics.

"OK, I digressed and apologize for that. What I don't apologize for is humor and laughter. That is something God gave to us, and you may as well get used to it today. I have a strong feeling we'll be doing a lot of it up there . . . here . . . well, you know what I mean. As it says in Job 8:21, 'He will yet fill your mouth with laughter and your lips with shouts of joy.' I like the shouting part too by the way."

If Dad was trying to put the group at ease, it wasn't working, yet. But knowing Greg Bagwell, he'd warm the crowd up pretty soon, regardless of the circumstances and unusual setting.

"So, you probably want to ask me, 'Why did you plan your own funeral before you even . . . You know . . . keeled over, kicked the bucket, bit the big one, whatever you want to call it?'"

Most were wondering about that exact question even if Dad hadn't asked the question.

"Well, the answer is a simple one. I've done this because of my unconditional love for each of you viewing this video today. My hope and prayer is that the purpose of this service will become more apparent as the service progresses, so hang in there with me. We're all in for an enjoyable ride today."

As he adjusted his collar on both sides forward with his hand (a habit I don't even think he was aware he had, another sign of his OCD), he leaned forward into the picture, almost becoming cartoonish on the screen with his head now dominating the big screen. "By the way, what do you think about this place – not the lake, but the theater you're in? One reason I selected this movie theater is that I spent a number of nights and afternoons with my family and my beautiful bride at this movie theater. Being able to bring Jared and Lindsey to see major motion pictures as they hit the big screen . . . shoot, we even hit a drive-in theater a couple of times when we had them in prior cities we lived in. Watching movies, being one of my most favorite things in life, experiencing life through the lens of so many creative people in the movie industry, had to make it part of today's event. Why not, right?" he inquired of the group as if it was a rhetorical question.

"Even though I thought about it because I love it, no popcorn will be served today. Sherri vetoed it actually. I was probably the only person eating popcorn at this theater at a sell-out crowd that watched

Mel Gibson's *The Passion of the Christ* on opening day back in 2004. Sherri was so embarrassed and kept whispering to me while elbowing me that I was making way too much noise. I truly was trying to be quiet and respectful, but guess, I wasn't succeeding. At any rate, I love theater popcorn and hope God has a ton of it in heaven. I'm hopeful He has butter and a big saltshaker for me too. For those that have ever been to the movies with me, you know that I fill up a courtesy cup with salt and dip my popcorn into the salt with each handful of the delightful kernels of popped corn. And it obviously didn't clog my arteries although many thought it had something to do with my one kidney stone a few years ago." Dad chuckled at himself at this one.

"I'm digressing again, sorry!" he apologized, but I knew the digression was just a part of his being, typical of his thought process.

I felt like Dad was right there with me, talking in his typical, and sometimes random, style. He was all over the board and not overly methodical at times. That trait always seemed inconsistent with his perfectionism and OCD "tendencies," as he liked to say. He could be compared to one of the kids in the Family Circus cartoon, the one that took the long way on a short route, enjoying all life had along the way. That or the ball in a pinball machine, lighting things up along the way, but who knew where he'd bounce to next. That was the character talking to us here today from the big screen.

"Well, I don't want to take up your whole day, so let's move on. At this point, I've asked a few folks to come up to talk about Christ. That's right, not about Greg Bagwell but about Christ. They were instructed that they could say a little about me, but let's face it, the focus of today for everyone here needs to be Jesus Christ and the hope that each of you can have in Him. Whether I'm there today or not, my greatest desire is to have a reunion with every single individual in this theater within the next eighty years or so. It gives me chills now just thinking about how awesome it will be, beyond anything that any of us could possibly imagine. I love you all and, at this point, am turning the service over to the group of individuals who will be talking to you today. Please listen intently and take their words into the core of your being – your soul and your heart. Thanks."

As the screen faded to black, the lights were turned up slowly, revealing a podium that had been placed at the front of the theater at the base of the big screen. In preparation of this day's events, Dad had given me five rather large, two-foot-by-three-foot covered paintings that he'd finished, and he had scripted what he wanted me to say with each introduction of those who would be speaking today. Since I was generally the least emotional of our immediate family, I guess Dad figured that I could pull this emcee position off, no matter what. For the most part, he had been dead-on, no pun intended. Since my night-blindness had been getting progressively worse, I knew I'd struggle seeing inside the theater even if lights were just slightly dimmed, so I'd brought my own flashlight to guide my path to and from the podium. I felt like a theater usher for the day. Given that my retinal disease (with the hearing impairment) was named Usher syndrome, it seemed strangely befitting that I donned a flashlight like a theater usher. In my case, it wasn't to provide warnings to patrons who were unruly but rather so the light could guide my path, and I wouldn't trip over something, which was guaranteed to happen without a lighted path.

I clicked on the flashlight and guided my path to retrieve the first painting from the five I'd positioned against the front auditorium wall, handed it to one of my teenage cousins, Kyle, who carefully placed it on an easel that had been positioned in the center of the room. Each of the paintings was covered in black felt, and Kyle's job was to position each painting and unveil each after I read Dad's scripted introductions. My subtle nod was intended to be his signal to remove or place the appropriate painting on the easel or remove and carefully position said painting off to a side wall so as to not mix them up with one another.

I walked back to the podium, took my place, and addressed the group. "Dad asked me to introduce each of the five individuals that will be providing a form of eulogy today. As Dad stated, these won't be typical eulogies since the focus will be on Him with a capital H. As you may have noticed, I've placed a painting in the middle of the room with the help of my able assistant and cousin, Kyle. Dad completed these paintings for each of the individuals who will be presenting today. They haven't seen these paintings. These are intended to help them ensure that the focus today is on Jesus Christ instead of Greg Bagwell. As Dad told me, each painting will make sense to each individual when they see them, and it will ensure they focus on his Lord and Savior." By this, I'd started perspiring. I wasn't sure if it was because of anxiety or if I was just really missing Dad with my emotions running high.

"First up," I continued to read, "Renee Chapman, one of Dad's cousins." At this, I nodded, and Kyle unveiled the first painting, and the same painting appeared magically on the big screen, filling up the large space.

Renee had already started walking toward the podium and was prepared to speak, knowing she was first up in the batting order. But when the black velvet was removed by Kyle and she saw the painting, she stopped in her tracks. She covered her mouth with both hands and, after studying the painting for a brief moment, burst out laughing. Not the reaction I'd expected, but I supposed there was a story behind the picture that we'd better understand in short order.

The painting was of a country scene, in what looked like a dirt yard, in front of a relatively small shack of a house. There was an old tractor in the background; there appeared to be a ditch in the foreground with an unstable-looking plank walkway across it, a barn in the background, which had seen better days, a couple of chickens running amok, and the focal point of the painting, three dirty, barefoot kids that seemed to be involved in a mock wedding.

The veil on the chubby young curly-haired blonde girl appeared to be salvaged netting from a mosquito net or something, her bouquet made of yellow dandelions and long green slender leaves of some sort. She had on a makeshift off-white plain dress as her wedding gown that was obviously a few sizes too big for this young pale blonde girl. The brown-haired groom had a dandelion boutonniere as his only prop other than an adult's blue sport coat, white shirt, clip-on tie, and green pants. They stood in front of an old swing set with their arms interlocked for the ceremony. The preacher was the youngest of the threesome, looking like he might have been four or five years old. In his completely black outfit including shirt, pants, and tie, he held a big black Bible, and he had one arm outstretched in the air. With mouth open wide, the little dark curly-headed guy looked like he was preaching, but based on the scene, it appeared he was going through marriage vows with the elder playmates. None of the kids had on any shoes, which seemed appropriate for the country setting.

Renee reached the podium and once again looked back over her shoulder reflectively at the larger version of the painting on the big screen. She just shook her head and finally said in her slow and deliberate Southern accent, which seemed to add an extra syllable to half of her words, "Now, ain't that a hoot!"

More laughter rang from the audience, many of which knew Renee, and some who didn't know her from Adam (or Eve, for that matter). She continued, "Greg, you so crazy, 'n' I love you, cuz!" As she shrugged, she said, "I had my eulogy all ready 'n' I can assure you, it just went out the window." With that thought in mind, she crumpled up her notes and threw them on the floor. "Well, that takes care o' that!"

"OK. So let me set the scene here for ya'll," she said as she pointed to the painting displayed on the wall-to-wall movie screen. "That paintin' is the spittin' image of Greg, me, and Dom playin' in Grandad and Granny Rosie's front yard in Ar'kin'saw. For ya'll city folk, you ain't lived till you play'd in the country with little to no toys other 'n your own hands 'n' a ton of imagination." Now we knew who was in the picture, but not much beyond that. What was Dad really trying to accomplish with these paintings? I knew there was a method to his madness, but I was beginning to wonder if he'd really thought through how this would play out.

"Dom's the preacher, which obviously makes Greg the groom 'n' me the bride. We had more fun playin' in that yard at Judd Hill. That's what we called this part of town just outside of Truman, Ar'kin'saw." She evidently hadn't noticed the ditch yet as she squealed, "Oh my gosh 'n' he's even got the ditch 'n there, ya'll. That's just wild. He didn't leave a single detail out."

"Well, Greg asked us to talk 'bout Jesus, 'n' this oil paintin' tells me 'xactly what Greg wanted me to talk 'bout today. First off, this was our grandparents' home, Granddad and Granny Rosie's place, where they raised their brood of kids, a bunch of which are here today, some of the best aunts and uncles this side of the Mason-Dixon Line."

"If ya'll noticed" – as she pointed at the painting on the easel – "Greg has painted this here beam of light that is shinin' down on that big ole fam'ly Bible that Dominic is holdin.'"

She smiled as she seemed to be reading Dad's mind on what he wanted us to hear. "That Bible's been in the Bagwell fam'ly for prob'ly a century. It's more than symbolic as Granddad and Granny Rosie drilled it into our heads – the Bible, that one in particular, was the most prized possessions they had. It was what guided them in raisin' the Bagwell clan, but more importantly, it's God's words that helped save more than a gen'ration of fam'ly. It was the only Bible we know'd of in that house, and it was to be respected and revered." She pursed her lips, looked up in the air, sighed, and then continued, "It was read aloud often and set the way this fam'ly lived their life. Not that there wouldn't be times when folks didn't stray 'way from the truth, but if I heard it one time, I heard it a hundred times, 'Train up a child in the way he should go, 'n' when he is old, he will not depart from it.' That's Proverbs 22:6 – one of the many scriptures that Granddad made sure we memorized at an early age."

As Renee took another moment to reflect here, I recalled stories that Dad had told of times past where a number of these aunts and uncles were pretty rebellious, doing their own thing and whooping it up, as he used to say. They seemed to be good, moral people who, if salvation was based on works, they'd probably make it to heaven. But many walked the aisle of churches in their twenties and thirties, fully "surrendering" their lives, making what they called a public profession of faith. Based on my years with this family, one thing impressed me: this family either didn't lose their sense of humor after becoming Christians or they developed one as a result. Either way, I did not see that as a consistent trait within the Christian community; many seemed to be miserable after their salvation experiences, from my observations.

One story that Dad had shared with me about his family was about his uncle Ruben, who to me was one of the most humble, loving, and quiet people I'd known in my life to that point. The only thing I saw that he did that could have qualified as sin was smoking. He was one of those three-pack-a-day guys that smoked nonfiltered Camel cigarettes for years. But I'd heard one of those country preachers down in Arkansas years ago say that "smokin' wouldn't send ya to hell, it'd just make ya smell like ya been there." As a result of this statement from the country preacher, I figured Ruben was pretty safe.

I heard from other family, though, that when he walked the aisle at a tent revival meeting way back in the 1960s, he uncharacteristically was shouting and waving his hands in the air, pleading with God to forgive him of all his sins and that he knew that the only way to salvation was through Jesus. He even fell at the altar in the front of the tent that had been temporarily set up for the weeklong event and hit his head on the old wooden altar, knocking himself out. By the time he came to, he was asking if he was in heaven to which a bunch of folks just laughed and told him, "Not yet, Ruben, not yet, but you got your ticket now." Dad said he was "born again" that night. There must have been a born again movement sweeping across the country back in that decade because I didn't seem to hear much about being "born again" these days.

Renee continued, "I can tell ya'll ... There was a bunch of us who did stray 'way, but jus' like it says in Isaiah 53:6, 'We all, like sheep, have gone astray, each of us has turned to his own way.'" At this, Renee put her hand on her hip and looked downward as if to stress the next piece of knowledge that we all needed to know. "Don't know if ya'll know, but sheep 'er one of the dumbest animals there is ... It's int'restin' that we're referred to as sheep so much in scripture. Just like what I've seen with sheep in the country, they blindly follow, and on occasion, they stray 'way from the pack, usually 'cause somethin's got their attention. Jus' like with us ... We see somethin' that gets our attention, and we go off the path, followin' stuff that ain't good for us and will lead us to destruction just like with the sheep. We'd follow another sheep right off a cliff like one of them there lemmins', none of us realizin' the danger that we're in or puttin' others in."

She shivered as she continued, "Gives me goosebumps jus' thinkin' 'bout it. Once sheep get it that their shepherd's there to protect 'em, they become completely loyal and rarely stray 'way anymore. A picture of the way we are once we realize that Christ loves us so much that he laid down his life for us, 'n' our complete devotion and loyalty to Him ultimately saves us, regardless of what may be tryin' to lure us 'way from Him."

She paused again, gathering some thoughts as she pensively looked again at the painting. "Ya know, I almost forgot what the three of us was doin' before that play weddin'. We had us a funeral for a frog." She giggled. "Know it sounds funny, but we had what I'll call a little ve-hic-u-lar homicide that mornin' with a bicycle." That caused laughter as most of us created a mental picture of the scene.

"Greg wasn't able to ride those big bikes, but he tried to with Aunt Patsy's and run'd right over a frog before he got half way 'cross the yard. He was so upset, being Mr. Sensitive City Boy. And I'll tell what's the truth . . . The frog weren't too happy 'bout it neither. Greg said he'd never killed nothin' before. Dom and I was crackin' up, ya'll, 'cause it was just a frog, ya know. But what I saw in Greg that day was a compassion 'n' love for God's cre-a-tion, and it made me realize right then 'n' there that God loves us so much more to a point of givin' up his Son to die in our place on that cross some two thousand years ago."

As she further reflected, she continued, "I remember Dom on that day. Shoot, that boy couldn't read a lick at that age, but he opened that big ole Bagwell fam'ly Bible – that no one knew we had out there, by the way – 'n' he pretended to read the twenty-third psalm. Greg 'n' I was cryin' with laughter and as Dom kept gettin' louder with his preachin', he was getting more and more upset with us, but he finally completed the psalm. Then he went straight into "Now I lay me down to sleep, I pray the Lord my soul to keep" to which Greg and I lit'rely fell on the ground, holdin' our stomachs as we rolled in that wonderful ole dirt yard. Now that I think about it, I think we invented ROFL."

"Dom thought we was makin' fun of him, and he got so mad at us he threw the fam'ly Bible down in the dirt and ran off to the house cryin' like a baby to tell on us for makin' fun of him. That stopped Greg 'n' I in our tracks, not 'cause we was afraid of gettin' in trouble, but 'cause we saw that precious fam'ly Bible sittin' in the dirt all twisted and crumpled up. We just knew that it was damaged, big-time. But sure as I'm standin' here today, that Word of God withstood even Dominic's tantrum. Greg 'n' I snuck it back into Granddad and Granny Rosie's house and never told no one what we'd done, that is, till today." Evidently, some of the Bagwell family understood the significance of that family Bible as they let out a combined laugh and gasp as if a family treasure had been breached, but still humored by the picture of the story that Renee had articulated so well.

Renee stopped for a moment and held up what looked like a huge worn black Bible and closed with, "This . . . this . . . I had no idea Greg was gonna have that paintin' there, but this is that fam'ly Bible. I brought it with me here today 'cause Greg wanted us to talk more 'bout Christ. This Bible represents the gen'rations of Bagwells that have and will continue to give their lives to Christ." You could tell that people were amazed that she had produced that Bagwell family Bible from what seemed like thin air. I wondered if Dad had asked Renee to bring the Bible, but I suppose it could have been some kind of coincidence.

"This is the legacy that ever'one here should be known for, just like Granddad and Granny Rosie did, a legacy of leadin' entire generations to a savin' grace and etern'l life in heav'n. I know one thing for sure . . ." She looked upward and addressed Dad, "Greg Bagwell, you ole coot, you gonna be havin' some kinda reunion with those two and I have a strange suspicion that you might even see a familiar frog up there."

At this, Renee grabbed that big Bible and started toward her seat.

Kyle, as if on cue, walked over, removing the first painting and placing the next covered painting in its place. This was my queue to get up to introduce the next person.

# CHAPTER 14

AS I WALKED toward the podium with flashlight in hand, I glanced around at the friends and family that had gathered here, and they looked much more relaxed at this unusual format for a funeral, but for some reason, I was actually feeling a little more uneasy. I looked around, wiped a little dampness from my brow with a handkerchief, something I rarely had on me but did today, probably in case someone else needed it, and readied myself for the next introduction.

"Our next person to speak is my dad's uncle on his dad's side, Uncle RT." Short and sweet introductions from now on for me since the format of the event was now established.

As the agile seventy-five-year-old uncle made his way up to the podium, I nodded to Kyle, who removed the second black velvet covering from another painting that he'd already placed on the easel in the front of the auditorium. Simultaneously, the same painting appeared in its full glory on the big screen. Uncle RT knew the drill now, knowing that a painting would be unveiled, so he didn't react en route.

But when he did arrive at his designated spot at the podium, he took his own handkerchief and dabbed his eyes ever so slightly. This tall, slender distinguished-looking gentleman could have passed for sixty with no problem. He took a deep breath, which could be heard and seen from almost anywhere in the room and slowly spewed the air out from his bottom lip. He then tapped on the microphone twice to make sure it was working. It was and we heard. *Twunk, twunk.*

"Well, I guess Greg knew what he was doin' when he asked me up here, but I'm much more comfortable with small crowds and not addressing a group from a podium. So I'll do what makes me comfortable with all of you and picture all of you in your underwear." There were a few surprised looks and a bunch of giggles from the Bagwell clan, who never knew what to expect with RT.

Then, with an unsettled look of disgust on his face, he added, "Oh my gosh, Brenda . . . I don't think that's appropriate undergarments for a lady of your age," pointing directly at his sister-in-law. She let out a huge laugh, crossing her arms as if to prevent RT from even attempting to go any further. Once others realized she thought this was funny, they laughed as well.

RT then said, "Now I think I'm OK, and I know for those of you that know me realize that is debatable." A few more chuckles.

"Well," he said as he pointed at the painting and the big screen, "I now understand why Renee threw her notes away . . . 'cause Greg threw me off here as well."

"Since he asked us to focus on Christ versus him, I think I know what he was wanting me to get across to you, based on that amazing painting. The only painting I've gotten from Greg till now is of an elephant. It's good, but this . . ." He pointed toward the screen, adding, "This . . . is just . . . ah . . . well, unbelievable!"

The painting was of a much younger version of Uncle RT, sitting on an old dock at a pond, with a kid that looked to be about thirteen or fourteen, fishing off the old dock that had seen better days. In white T-shirts and jeans rolled up to their knees, they were both dangling their feet over the edge, partially in the water. The young teen had one of his legs crossed underneath his other leg. The man was pulling the kid's cap down over his face while the kid (who I assumed was Dad) had a broad smile and nearly bent over double with arms flailing about in uncontrolled laughter, both apparently having a joyful moment in the great outdoors.

It appeared that they were unaware of a fish that they'd hooked as you could see a bass had broken the water with the end of the fishing line from one of their poles obviously hooked in its mouth. The red-and-white bobber and fishing line formed a wavy pattern all the way out to the largemouth fish, which was airborne about a foot above the pond's surface. A net lay on the dock, and a small dark green rusty-looking metal tackle box sat next to it.

The two men depicted in the painting were oblivious to anything other than each other, a serene setting with still water and a perfect mirror image reflection of the woods on the opposite side of the body of water. Small ripples around the fish that had just jumped were starting to form, and you could envision them growing larger once the fish landed back into the water with a splash. Vibrant colors of blue and yellow wild flowers and white and pink blossoms on the trees and bushes surrounding the scene would lead one to believe the setting to be early spring.

What caught my attention most were the expressions on the two faces, which could only be described as a devout love for each other. Even the heavens seemed to agree, given a penetrating light that peered through the clouds in the sky, casting direct light on the two as they clowned around in the pond scene.

RT, after soaking in the painting for a brief few seconds, looked directly at the audience and said, "Well, I'm sure you figured out that the good-lookin' guy in the picture is me." Laughter rippled through the audience. "What you may not know," he added as he pointed and chuckled, "is the honery-lookin' youngster there is Greg Bagwell."

"One would think that if he was going to do a self-portrait, he'd make it a little more flattering, don't ya think?" He paused, looking off toward a side wall of the auditorium while squinting his eyes and scrunching up his face. He'd placed his hand up to his face while placing two fingers directly over his lips in pensive thought. He then moved his hand over his nose and slid the hand down, opening his mouth to speak as his hand passed over his mouth, as he pointed indiscriminately toward the picture on the big screen.

"Let me describe this scene and how it points to Christ since I know Greg didn't want our focus today to be on him."

RT continued, "This was a fairly familiar scene with the two of us around this time of life . . . I'd guess it would be around 1972. Greg and I spent a lot of weekend days out at Busch Wildlife just outside of St. Charles, Missouri, doing what he enjoyed for recreation, fishing. My guess is Greg was depicting a time shortly after his dad, who was my older brother, Shelby, passed away. His mom was still alive, but I had committed to Shelby to help fill his shoes with Greg after he was gone. I so enjoyed fulfilling that commitment, spending time with Greg. This was never work but rather a pleasure to serve my brother as well as little Greggy-boy"

In many ways, I felt like I knew my grandfather that RT spoke of . . . Shelby. Dad's father was a real man's man. He was a rugged outdoorsman who loved hunting, fishing and hiking. Dad was the middle child of three – his brother, Gene, being the oldest, and his sister, Faye, the youngest. The two boys were only twenty months apart, and Faye was the "planned accident," as his mother and father had put it. They were thrilled to finally give birth to a daughter, and Faye became the apple of their eye. Although they loved each of their children equally, they seemed to have more time and resources for their little girl. Dad always said he was OK with this, but I always sensed it bothered him to some degree, probably one more brick he stacked up on the wall he'd created in his life.

Dad tended to stuff his emotions for years, not letting others know of any form of pain or hurt he experienced in his life. This didn't work very well for him, though, and even though he "walked the aisle" as a young child, he continued relying on his own strength, wisdom, and power for many years. That was the case until he finally met the one thing that he couldn't control, which also seemed to ease his pain – alcohol and drugs. At one time, he'd become convinced that the abusive substances saved his life. He would later admit that it began to slowly choke the life from him.

My grandfather, Shelby, became ill in his late thirties, doctors saying that rheumatoid arthritis, combined with major degenerative discs were primary culprits. After three major back surgeries by the age of thirty-nine, he was told that he could never lift over five pounds again. For a man who made a living as a flight mechanic for an airline manufacturer with just an eighth grade education, it forced him into early disability. He never really regained his strength as he hobbled around with a walking cane and dropped some forty-five pounds after the last surgery, which was the one that did him in. At a mere 145 pounds at nearly six foot, Grandpa Bagwell was unable to tolerate the constant daily pain without medicating himself with painkillers. The doctor continued to try experimental drugs for the arthritis and prescribed as many of the numbing drugs as Grandpa felt he needed. Dad said the "killer" in "painkiller" was an accurate description as he was convinced these medications were mostly responsible for his dad's death.

Grandpa Bagwell was diagnosed with kidney failure at forty years of age, and one short year later, after several attempts at preparing him for dialysis, his vital organs began to shut down quickly, one by one, and he died quietly at home in his sleep, just shy of his forty-first birthday. His children were young to be without a parent, ranging in age from three to fifteen. Dad found out years after his father's death that RT had stepped in to act as a surrogate father to him and his older brother after Shelby passed away. Although he knew the role RT filled, he didn't know about the unwritten pact between his dad and his uncle. Faye just clung to her mother at the tender age of three, becoming the shadow of Eva Mae, a godly woman who lived a content and peaceful life for years to come.

Dad's brother, Gene, was an independent kid, and at fifteen, he was much more interested in spending time with his friends than family. Given the good group of kids he hung with, RT wasn't worried. Gene had been involved with youth group at church, and his friends all were part of that group.

Greg, like his siblings, was close to his dad, but he hadn't gotten as involved with any youth group at church and needed a father figure in his life, which both Eva Mae and Shelby realized before Shelby's untimely death. Dad was more interested in outdoor activities, and being with his dad was more than sufficient for him before his passing. Dad knew that his father was becoming more frail, sensing he was more ill than the family let on. So he spent as much time with him as he could in those last few years. His sense of impending loss was correct, and he lost his best friend, his dad, at age thirteen.

RT knew that Greg didn't have a core group of friends nor were there other father figures to help him through this difficult time. He found himself spending time with Greg on weekends, fishing and hiking, two of Dad's favorite pastimes. Dad wouldn't have known it, but RT could have cared less about either activity, but his uncle knew he was making an investment in his nephew and fulfilling a promise made to his elder brother as well.

It wasn't until Greg had started his freshman year in college that he started withdrawing from RT and started to spend more and more time with his fraternity brothers. This time became a time of weaning off his uncle but also a time of partying and sowing his wild oats. Greg smoked his first joint during rush week, and it became a regular substance, the relaxing effects of which were like no other for him.

Taking him away from the harsh realities of life, he made pot smoking a regular habit. He advanced quickly, and within two months of his first joint, he bought his first bag of pot. He rationalized the purchase in his mind that he didn't want to continue to bum the "stuff" off others. The reality was that he was hooked, not so much due to an addiction, but rather to the escape. Since smoking marijuana wasn't always convenient or acceptable in certain crowds, he began drinking, moving quickly from beer to hard liquor. He liked the effect and immediately fell in love with the warmth he'd get as the warm liquid made its way down his throat, followed by that wondrous dulling effect. He started to drink the hard stuff straight out of the bottle in order to feel the effect quicker, but this was hidden as he knew this wasn't normal among his circle of friends. The dullness of senses made him feel like he was more in control than he actually was. He found that he felt more like he "fit in" with others and didn't have fear of being around anybody as long as he was "lit" in one way or another. Inhibitions became a thing of the past.

During this first year of college, RT had sensed that Dad was beginning to transition from the security of being around his uncle to finding friends his own age. As a result, RT pulled away at what he believed an appropriate pace to give his nephew some space. Space was an appropriate word as that's where Dad seemed most comfortable away from reality and in some space far away. It wasn't until many years later that he advanced to prescription drugs and cocaine. He knew he had a fear of coke and should have known that his fear of getting hooked was an early indicator of his genuine concern of having an addictive personality.

Even with RT pulling away and giving Dad space at that time, the bond between them didn't go away, and it never would. Dad knew that his uncle loved him and also knew that he was one of the few people he actually trusted. He had a sense that if you loved something too much, it would be taken away as with his own dad, so he continued life in a guarded manner, except with this special uncle. Even with the trust that he had with his uncle RT, he was still fearful of letting him in on his dependence on substance, just one more indicator that he actually did have a problem.

"There had been a special bond between the two of us from the time he came into the world, but we grew even closer after his dad, Shelby, passed on." He gazed at the picture while he spoke. "What really just comes off the canvas of Greg's painting for me is the lighting." He shook a pointed finger toward the picture as he continued. "The light that is shining on us from the clouds in that painting symbolizes to me that God's hand was on both of us, especially during that time, giving me wisdom to be a parental figure to Greg and for Greg to allow joy back into his life."

"I could never replace his dad . . . my brother . . . but God knew that we needed each other."

"I wasn't saved when Shelby died, but having this new responsibility and feeling the weight of Greg's eternal destination on my shoulders . . . It got me thinking and finally got me to do something about it." He smiled broadly at this, adding, "That kid had more impact on my eternal destination than I ever had on his."

He teared up but was maintaining his composure as he said, "God is good, folks. If you aren't sure of your eternal destiny, firm that up before you leave here today. Greg wanted to make sure God's Word was spoken here today, so let me quote an appropriate scripture about God's love and his desire for you being a part of His kingdom. As it says in Romans 8:39, "'Neither height nor depth, nor anything else in all creation, will be able to separate us from the love of God that is in Christ Jesus our Lord.'"

"This is what Greg wanted me to say today, I'm convinced. That we need to experience the love of Christ and that each and every one of us can play more of an impact on others that we can possibly imagine. I know Greg had no idea that he was one of the primary reasons for me making the most important decision of my life . . . the decision to accept Jesus Christ as my personal savior. That is not something that someone else can do for you, and you aren't born into the Christian family. It is only found through asking Christ into your own heart and turning from your sin. There is only one way, and that way is Jesus"

He wrapped up by saying, "So look at the painting up there," pointing at the painting that appeared on the big screen. "Note the love, note the warmth, and know that God is smiling from above at the fact that he can speak to us in many ways. We just need to be open and listen for Him. He loves you and wants you to be one of His, just as Greg and I both became His."

Looking upward, RT closed out his comments. "It's gonna be one unbelievable time of celebration when we all get there," and as he looked back toward the audience, he added one final comment and command. "Do *not* miss it!"

# CHAPTER 15

**K**YLE HAD TO be nudged this time by his mom, Faye, and he darted over to the easel, removing the painting of Uncle RT and Dad and with fluid motion, gathered up the next painting and placed it on the easel. His foot caught the easel as he started toward his seat, but the agile youngster dropped and rolled instead of allowing his heavy foot to topple the easel and painting. He stood up, wiped his brow with the back of his hand, and with eyes wide, eyebrows almost touching his dark mane of hair atop his head, pursed his lips in a whistling like form while mouthing "whew." Only a few people toward the front of the auditorium noticed Kyle's near miss and recovery. One of the youngest of Faye's blurted out a full single laugh, which Faye stopped quickly with one stern glance from her toward Craig, Kyle's little brother.

I had already made my way to the podium, and due to my night-blindness and poor peripheral vision, which was continuing to deteriorate, I didn't see a thing. I paused and breathed out slowly as this next introduction was extra special for me, one of my best friends and someone I'd spent my life with, my sister, Lindsey. Or as we called her in her younger days, Lindz.

I cleared my throat and, once again, was feeling my emotions close to the surface more and more as the service progressed. "Thanks, Uncle RT. Our next person to grace the stage is someone I have known my entire life, a close friend and someone I share many common bonds with."

I'd gone off script by this time, and I knew Dad wouldn't mind as long as I didn't get too far off track. "A beautiful young lady, who happens to be my only sibling as well, Lindsey, or as a couple of us refer to her, Lindz Nelson."

Before I relinquished my position at the podium to my sister, I glanced over at the painting that Kyle had already positioned on the easel and smiled. Since I'd accidently walked in on Dad when he was completing this particular painting a few months ago, I was really excited to see how Sis would respond.

As soon as Lindsey got up from her seat and started toward the podium, Kyle slid the black cover away from the piece. Lindsey never broke her stride as she strode to the podium, more due to her own night-blindness that was surfacing than due to her being in control. She looked amazing in a three-quarter-length navy maternity dress. It was a simple classic wool dress with long sleeves in an empire cut with a number of pleats that gave room for expansion for the upcoming months. Silver jewelry accented her attire, and it was just enough, not too much to detract from the beauty of her outfit or her own natural beauty. Her highlighted blonde hair was pulled up in a loose bun, and she looked stunning.

She seemed a little nervous when she got in front of the crowd, and even with my limited sight, I could see the glistening of a tear streaming down her cheek. That was enough to cause my own eyes to start watering, but I knew I needed to maintain composure in case she glanced my way. But after her bright brilliant blue eyes met her husband's, she gained the confidence she needed to move forward as she slowly and inconspicuously wiped her cheek as dry as possible with her hand. Though not visible, I knew she'd tucked a handkerchief on a shelf of the podium prior to the start of today's event as a precaution and just in case her emotions got the best of her.

As with the others, the painting had been something that seemed to add a twist to what they had intended to say this November morning but didn't change the focus, which Dad had made clear to each of them. *Keep the focus on Christ!* That had been his simple guidance to each of the five that would be speaking today.

Lindsey first addressed the friends and family. She then turned her attention in pensive thought toward the painting.

"Thank each of you for coming today. Dad would have been impressed that this movie theater, one of his favorite places to spend time watching flicks, actually became a reality for this service. It's a good thing drive-in movie theaters are a thing of the past 'cause I have a feeling you'd be sitting in your cars right now listening through those funny little speakers that didn't seem to work any better than the primitive drive-through restaurant speaker systems." With this, several of the babyboomers laughed at the nostalgic thought, and one could tell that they were grateful for indoor theaters as well.

Lindz and I had only been to a handful of drive-in theaters as kids, which Dad had found years ago near our home in Naperville, Illinois, where we spent only three years of our lives together. Lindsey and I both felt like we'd walked onto a set of some '50s sitcom the few times we had the privilege to go to the drive-in theater, and we loved the experience. We were saddened when they closed the drive-in with seemingly no notice but rather with a clear message with chains draped across the entrance and exits. Although we begged Dad to help us find another drive-in theater to further enjoy the nostalgic movie experience, we could no longer find any operable in the southwestern Chicago suburbs. It was as if the few remaining outdoor movie theaters closed around the country in the late '90s, but we did believe there to be a handful still in remote areas around the country, just not anywhere around us as best we knew.

Lindsey continued, "I am so proud to be a part of today's events and, after having a glance at the surprise painting, feel that Dad must have seen my notes as there is a direct link between my notes and this painting."

At this, she paused and took a moment to gaze up at the big screen while arranging her notes which appeared to be on index cards, which she'd conveniently placed on the podium shelf as well. Given her background as a second grade elementary school teacher, the cards seemed out of character, more reserved for someone used to making business speeches as opposed to an elementary school teacher. I wouldn't have been surprised if she had pulled out wide-lined off-white pages on which elementary school children often practiced writing the alphabet but was surprised at the sight of index cards. Minimally, I would have expected them to be neon colored to match her occupation as an elementary school teacher.

Lindsey held her index cards as she turned toward the original oil painting to reflect on the scene once again. The painting was a picture of a young blonde woman pushing one of those three-wheeled jogging strollers with a giddy-looking toddler, who walked between her and a short young blonde man. She was holding the finger of a muscular young man with her free hand in between the couple. The young child was pointing upward at dozens of pastel-colored balloons that apparently had been turned loose as they were floating upward into the air.

The backdrop scene appeared to be Navy Pier, a popular downtown Chicago attraction, with a giant Ferris wheel as the most dominant feature outside of a group of boat attractions on the opposite side of the painting on the shore of Lake Michigan. The Seadog and Odyssey were two of the most recognizable water attractions on the lake on the other side of the boardwalk, one a fast, bouncy way to see the city from the lake while the other "sea vessel" more reserved for formal evening events, including dancing and fine dining. The other prominent feature of the painting was the long building just beyond the Ferris wheel that house a myriad of souvenir and specialty shops, IMAX theater, and a number of restaurants. A handful of street vendors with carts, selling anything from popcorn to lemonade, were positioned along the boardwalk in front of the elongated building. A favorite summer attraction to visit in the city.

In looking at the details of the painting, one was forced to follow the direction of where the toddler was pointing. Even though balloons seemed to be what had captured the child's attention, there was something else that the artist was trying to get the viewer to notice. A lone man who appeared to be somewhat transparent sat in one of the Ferris wheel carriages toward the top of the wheel. Since Dad had added a light fog over the entire picture, the man was even harder to detect without closer inspection. The ghostlike image of the man was leaning forward in the Ferris wheel car, with his head and elbows resting on the arm rail. Based on the contentment and smile that permeated his face and given the direction he was looking, he appeared more interested in the scene of the young family than the wonderful views of the city that one could get from this lofty vantage point. On what appeared to be a summer day, it was a quite colorful picture and brought back a lot of memories of downtown trips as a kid for both the Bagwell children.

Lindsey gathered her thoughts and, still looking toward the painting, said, "Well, Dad," as if addressing the gentleman in the car on the Ferris wheel, "you really know how to capture moments of yesterday and tomorrow in a way that tugs at the heartstrings."

By now, she was unusually calm, cool, and collected today, especially under the circumstances, let alone with the hormonal imbalance pregnancy can add to an emotional day like this.

"Let me describe what this painting means to me, which I also believe was the intention of Dad's brush as he stroked this canvas."

"Dad knew that we (Jared and I) loved these downtown trips from the far western rural suburbs. Especially places like Navy Pier and the museums, where not only we, but where Dad could be a kid." Smiles throughout the audience confirmed that Dad did indeed like to be a kid himself.

She continued, "This picture is depicting a time that is yet to happen, I'm quite certain of that." As she pointed at the large screen, she added, "That's John and me, along with our beautiful daughter that I'm now carrying, and the setting . . . Well, those of you from Chicagoland know that it's Navy Pier in downtown Chicago along the lakefront."

Looking back in the vicinity of where her husband, John, was sitting, she spoke directly to John. "For the record, Mr. Nelson, Dad did a great job of capturing 'her' – little Hannah, that is." Lindsey's emphasis being on "her." Those who knew John's relentless reference to their unborn "son" knew exactly what she was getting at, and she looked at the painting as a premonition, a foreshadowing of the sex of their firstborn. Those close enough to the couple to know of their little battle of the sexes let out a giggle, even more so when John waved his hand at her in a "whatever" gesture. John's Mom even said a little louder than intended, "You got that right, girl," which brought on even more laughter. Her mother-in-law reeled back, covering her mouth with her hands, realizing her thoughts had been audibly heard. Oops. Lindsey didn't miss a beat with what could have become a distraction and just continued.

"What I'm also seeing in this wonderful painting is that Hannah is not just pointing at a bunch of balloons, which was always a favorite of mine at that age, but also at the distinguished gentleman on the Ferris wheel. He's a little hard to make out in the painting since he's not in focus. However, in case you're still wondering, I'm convinced that represents Dad, who..." She choked up for the first time but regained her composure quickly and continued, "Who won't actually be with us when we take that stroll along the boardwalk at Navy Pier."

"But," she added with confidence, "that man will be with us throughout eternity due to the redemptive power of our savior, Jesus Christ."

She lingered with a short pause. "Redemption." She paused again before continuing,

"Redemption – that word captures what I see in this painting. Dad was like the prodigal son, but I'd refer to him more as the prodigal father. He took a departure away from his Creator, his family, and friends, escaping from reality in search of something, anything that could take his pain away for a number of years. He thought he'd found it in drugs, in alcohol, in isolation, but you know what he found?

"He found emptiness, he found desperation, he found hopelessness, and he found loneliness."

Looking upward and raising one arm in obvious praise, she said, "All leading him back, humbled, patient, kind, loving – someone ready to stop trying to control everything, someone who you could almost see break into meekness before your very eyes."

While maintaining her sights upward and raising her arm even higher, she added, "A real man who was finally willing to surrender, who knew without a shadow of a doubt that he could no longer do life on his own. The wondrous redemption that Christ promises each of us if we simply do what Dad did: surrender to our savior, who sacrificed it all on a cross for our sins."

Almost preaching it now, she added, "So each and every person who has been and ever will be won't have to earn their way into heaven through their own goodness but through grace by faith . . . Redemption that cost us nothing, which cost Christ everything. The best free gift that any of us could ever hope and dream for.

"As it says in John 3:16, 'For God so loved the world that He gave His only begotten Son that whosoever believes in Him should not perish, but gain everlasting life.'"

She shivered, indicating that the impact of the verse meant something deep within her very being. "I don't know about you, but when we see the redemption story unfold in such a dramatic way as it did with my earthly dad, you know that no one is too far gone, no one has been too bad, and anyone can be redeemed. It is Christ that it speaks of in Colossians 1:14 when the Word says, 'In whom we have redemption, the forgiveness of sins.'"

She looked back at the painting one last time as she wrapped up her brief talk of redemption, which had become a virtual sermon. The whole time I listened, I realized that there was another person in this large auditorium that wasn't willing to turn it over yet and certainly not trusting the "big guy upstairs." The big guy sure didn't seem to be doing a very good job of things with our lives, as best I could tell, and that was just one of the reasons I wasn't ready to make any form of a commitment, at least at this point in my life.

"Dad, thanks for reminding me of the fact that we'll be spending eternity together because you, the prodigal father, returned, not to me, not to Mom, and not to Bud, but to your Creator, who has given you the ultimate inheritance. His arms were always open, waiting for you, no matter how far you got away from Him. Words cannot express how happy I am that you finally ran home to Him." She choked up again on the last few words but pulled it together as she concluded.

Almost as an afterthought and with a shift to lightheartedness, she said, "Oh yeah, and for foretelling a future story, showing how incredibly joyful we will be with our beautiful daughter, Hannah." Lindsey closed in light laughter from herself and from the audience. At this, I walked up toward Lindsey to give her a hug and escort her back to her seat, something Dad would have done (or at least would have told me to do).

Kyle had enough practice by this point in the ceremony that he had his part down pat, and he wasn't about to make another faux pas. He had already stepped over and picked up the next mystery painting veiled in black, walked it up to the easel a little more gingerly, removed the Navy Pier scene, and placed the new painting in its appropriate place. Based on the way he was handling his job for the day, he could apply with one of those art auctions. At least, that was my take, based on my only exposure of an art auction, which was on a family cruise a few years ago. Dad coerced us into sitting in on one of the cruise art auctions one night, and it was fairly entertaining. He purchased three prints that night to Mom's chagrin. She found an appropriate place for all three paintings once we returned home, though, the basement wall, which not all guests in our home would have seen. So much for buying fine art.

I walked up quickly after getting Lindsey seated back with her husband and began the next introduction, once again being short and sweet on the introduction, just as Dad had suggested.

# CHAPTER 16

"**O**UR NEXT PERSON to take the podium is one of Dad's best friends. Theirs is not a unique story, but one of devout and loyal friendship. Each one of us is very fortunate if we have one close friend that is like a brother in life, and that is certainly what JD Crawford has been to Dad, a friend closer than a brother . . . JD?"

JD was already on his way down to the front of the theater. He had a bounce to his step that always seemed to portray a joy in his life that many yearned for and which many never would experience. JD had a comfort of being in his own skin. He wore a bright smile that always had people wondering what he was up to, and the majority of time, he wasn't up to anything. In the upper Midwest, most people were suspicious of people who were this happy, figuring the person was up to something or worse yet, they wanted something. Some contingencies of people probably thought he was on something they wish they were on, but the reality was that JD, like Dad, he had been there, done that, and had the T-shirt in the closet to prove that he'd tried the substance scene. The simple truth was that there was little to really smile about during the height of his (or Dad's) addiction, but that had all changed. The interactions I'd had with JD made me realize that this was one of the real genuine guys, somebody who just loved life and loved people. I envied his happy-go-lucky attitude and believed it was attainable. I just wasn't exactly sure how to get it.

Like any other day, JD was dressed a little unusual for the occasion. He had on a pair of jeans, one of those ribbed collarless knit shirts (light tan), and he donned a brown suede sport coat. What outfit like this was complete without a pair of light tan pointed boots, right? Not his, for sure. JD was a fit man of about fifty, not unlike Dad. He had fairly long, salt-and-pepper wavy hair, and sported a goatee, making him look like a prominent and cool professor, which he wasn't. He had a liberated air about him that I know Dad admired, especially given Dad's more conservative nature. The only thing that seemed uncharacteristic to Dad's conservative nature was his shaven head. He almost looked like he had polished it as his head always had a shine to it, something I'd noticed lately that most balding guys have in common. It seemed that shaven heads were now in vogue, and even though I never asked Dad, I'm fairly certain that he did this not as a fashion statement but rather because it was a carefree style and cut down on time (a precious commodity in his last days) spent getting ready.

As JD was settling in at the podium, he began as he glanced over at the screen for the picture that he knew would be there. Kyle had already left the easel and realized by the blank screen and deafening silence that he hadn't pulled the black covering off the painting yet. In his haste to correct the error, he bolted back to the painting, yanked the black cover off, and nearly knocked the easel, painting and all to the floor. He steadied the easel with his free hand and, due to his quick action, avoided another near mishap. So much for his career at the art auction, but he was still doing a good job.

During the brief interlude, JD had propped his arms on the podium, resting his head in his open hands, and was patiently waiting for his cue – the introduction of the painting. He was gracious, but he couldn't resist having a little fun with it. "Well, I was beginning to believe Greg just painted a black canvass for me, which would have certainly challenged me to know what he was trying to get me to say to you all."

I don't think he'd even looked closely at the picture yet since he really had no reaction to the painting or the big screen replica that actually caused me to shiver (for some odd reason) when I saw it. I marveled at Dad's talent on many occasions, but this one seemed to jump off the canvas and literally tug at my heartstrings. Was I starting to get soft or what? I was struggling with figuring out what was happening with my emotions, which seemed to be all over the place these days, and in particular today. Understandably, I was shaken and out of sorts today due to that dreaded day the family had to go through the day before. Regardless, in the role I was fulfilling today, I had to stand firm and not visibly allow others to see how raw my emotions were today. There would be time at a later point where I could let my guard down. This was not that time.

JD looked at the painting on the big screen, and with his head raised, he pursed his lips and fought back his own emotion that had surfaced. Even though I wasn't close enough to see them, I sensed tears collecting in the corners of his eyes. I knew my suspicion was right when he took two fingers from each hand and wiped tears gently from his eyes. He was definitely touched by the painting. His reaction got me choked up again. *Stop it! I can't go there right now, so just stop! Think of something else . . . anything.* Although these were just thoughts, I was fearful that I'd blurt the words out as the words became so strong in my mind. My internal coaching must have been working as I was able to calm down somewhat and focus back on JD for the moment as well as the piece of art Dad had created that was before us.

The painting was fairly straightforward for anyone to understand. The setting appeared to be a river, with three men in the water that was up to their waists in gently moving waters. Two of the men each had one hand supporting the back of the man in the center, and the man on the left had a firm grip on the forearm of the central figure with his other hand. The man on the right, who was donned in what looked like a white robe, had his other arm raised high up in the air, and all three men had their eyes closed and heads raised toward the heavens. The man on the left and the central figure both had on what appeared to be plain black T-shirts. The dominant feature of the entire painting was rays of light that were coming out of clouds from the top right portion of the painting. The light was shining down on the man in the center, who seemed to be squatting in the shallow running waters while the other two seemed to have feet firmly planted on the riverbed, based on their upright posture. The streams of light made you know that this river baptism was something blessed from above, something that made the heavens open up and smile upon.

"Well, now that I've regained my composure for the moment, I know without a doubt what Greg was wanting me to share with you today . . . Let me sum it up in two words: grace and mercy."

"Before I get into the details of God's grace and mercy, let me talk a moment about that unbelievable moment depicted in the painting before you. The man in the center, in case you hadn't figured it out already, is me. The guy on the right is Ryan Dobbs, the head of men's ministry from Believer's Bible Chapel, and the guy on the left – that's our Greg. He assisted with the baptism that was done that day in Lake Geneva, Wisconsin. It was a cold November morning at a men's retreat that Greg 'made' me go to with him, which led to my own salvation. Little did I know what I was in for that day. If I'd known they weren't going to waste any time and make me go out into that frigid lake for a baptism at 9:00 in the morning, I probably would have stayed home that weekend." Laughter from around the auditorium could be heard as he continued, "But I can tell you one thing for sure. I am *soooo* glad I went and wouldn't trade that weekend for anything in the world."

"And let me tell you something . . . If you or a loved one don't know that you know that you know that your eternal destiny is locked down, rock solid, or if you think you or that loved one is too far gone to receive that wonderful free gift we all have just waiting for us, let me tell you a bit about what Christ pulled me up out of and, hopefully, you'll realize that nobody is too far gone."

I had learned to love people that my dad loved, and JD was one of those guys. But admittedly, he was just easy to love. He had an energy level and passion for life that was enviable, but I had to admit, he was losing me on some of this double-talk so far today. Maybe I just needed to pay closer attention so I could follow his line of thinking, so I listened more intently.

"I won't go through my entire life history . . . and some of you are thinking, good thing 'cause my stomach is starting to growl like a bear," which was interesting as it was already eleven twenty in the morning, and I hadn't even thought about food. That was until JD mentioned it; then my mind wandered for a moment, but I refocused when JD spoke again.

"But let me give you the *Reader's Digest* version," he said as he dove into the past.

"Like a lot of young kids, I decided the best way to not just be accepted during those strange years of adolescence but to be one of the really cool crowds was to start smoking anything I could get my hands on. Especially if it got me higher than a kite. I really believed I was the '70s equivalent of James Dean at Crystal Lake South High School and actually appeared to have it all, the brains, the brawn, and the girls. What more does a high school boy want, right?"

A rhetorical question, it seemed, but I had a feeling he was being sarcastic in his question.

"Even into college in the late '70s with free love and all the drugs and alcohol you could possibly imagine or desire, I still felt like the cat's meow. For you, younger guys and gals, that means I was really 'sick.'"

Laughter from the younger group of people rang from the audience and confused looks on most of the older people, thinking he meant something entirely different from the intended meaning. It always cracked me up when more mature adults used terms like this, though, because they didn't always use the word in exactly the appropriate context. This was no exception – we normally referred to things as being sick, not people. Oh well, most of us got the gist of what he meant.

JD continued, "Until that night that changed my life forever." He paused here and left us all hanging, wondering where in the world JD was going. "In the beginning of my senior year of college, I was driving home from a frat party, drunker than Cooter Brown and higher than the kite. It was around two o'clock in the morning, and the drive was only three to four miles back to campus where I was dropping off my date for the night, Leslie White."

I knew part of JD's story but don't think I'd heard about this particular night, so he was certainly piquing my interest.

One could tell that JD was reliving the experience as he retold the story that I'm sure he'd run through his memory bank a million times over.

"A deer, a big eight-point buck to be exact, ran out of the woods and froze in its tracks on the pavement in front of my car. It was about halfway back to campus on a rural road in DeKalb, Illinois. I not only couldn't make out what was in front of me but don't even remember what happened next . . . other than I woke up in a hospital and was in a load of pain. They wouldn't give me drugs as they probably figured I had more than enough painkilling substances in my system already. When I finally was able to comprehend things, they told me I'd swerved to avoid the deer and evidently wrapped my '71 Ford Mustang fastback around a large oak tree in front of someone's house." He barely took a breath as he told of this eventful night. "The crash had awoken the residents of the house, which was fortunate for me as I might not be standing here today if they hadn't woken up. Leslie wasn't so lucky . . . She died instantly in the crash."

Silence rang through the auditorium, and many were probably thinking similar questions that were running through my head, like "And you're not in prison?"

"You would think that a horrid event like this would finally be the wake-up call needed to change your life, but even with the prison stay over the next twelve years, I continued a downward spiral. I sunk into a deep depression, attempting suicide three times. One of those times, I came very close to succeeding. I was able to continue to get drugs and liquor in prison, though. Many people wonder how that can happen. All I can say is, there's a price, but you can get virtually anything in prison if you're willing to sell your soul."

How could this guy have a history like this and today seem so adjusted and content with his life. JD had a lot more skeletons in his closet than I ever imagined. I just knew him as one of Dad's step program buddies whom he'd grown very close to over the past few years of their mutual struggles with addiction. Never would I have guessed that JD had such a sordid past.

"When I got out of prison in '91, I was physically in the best condition of my life due to all the time we had on our hands in prison. It wasn't like there were a lot of other commitments during my prison stay. Emotionally and mentally, though, I was sick (not as in cool either). Even though I was able to complete my educational aspirations of completing a bachelor's degree while inside the three walls and bars of my cell, when released, I entered a world that was so completely unfamiliar to me. It scared me to death. Upon exiting the confines of prison after twelve long years, I wasted no time at all to ease my anxiety. I went straight to the liquor store, knowing I had little cash, but enough for a fifth of vodka."

"I drank the entire fifth straight out of the bottle that day in record time, feeling the soothing warmth that was so familiar to me and felt my shoulders relax, helping me adjust to this unusual world I was reentering. This became a key to me being able to cope with life outside of the pen. I would hold a few odd jobs here and there but was never able to hold on to a job for long. Reason being I'd eventually slip up and either show up drunk or high on a job or not show up at all and get fired."

This certainly didn't fit what I knew of JD, a man that had his own kitchen and bath remodeling business, an entrepreneur who seemed to have more business than his fair share. JD was known for his integrity, honesty, and fair deals in his line of business. He did very little advertising of his company, from what I understood, mostly gaining business from word of mouth and referrals, much like Dad. It didn't hurt either that he had a great sense of creative style and could listen to anyone's description of their remodeling need and crystallize their random thoughts into the perfect makeover. It seemed to most customers that he could read their mind's dreams for each unique job. I would never have guessed JD had such a horrific past, amazing me all the more today. How could he be the same man that he was describing today?

"In '98, I had gotten my second DUI in twelve months, only having had my license back to drive for two years. I should have had a dozen more, and that's probably understating it, but this time, they were taking my license from me and sending me back to prison if I didn't get help from my addiction demons. Among a few other fees and requirements, their remedy for me was a required twelve-step program, which I was completely sold on and knew I needed . . . NOT!"

JD knew he was going over his allotted time, so he looked out and quickly accelerated his story to get to the punch line.

"That required a series of meetings, which I was required to attend for ninety days, entailed getting a signature from the leader of each meeting seven days a week. Ninety in ninety, as us non-normee drunks call it. All I cared about was getting the signatures, filling my requirement, and making sure to be more cautious when driving high and/or drunk in the future."

He reflected on Dad at this point. "Greg was one of the leads at one of those meetings, and he told me that he was refusing to sign my attendance card until he could speak to me privately. The guy had the gall to call me on the carpet, saying that if I continued to come to meetings high, he would continue to refuse his John Henry on my time card, as I called it." He shrugged, throwing his hands up to demonstrate his past disgust, adding, "How dare the guy. Who did he think he was anyway?"

If he'd been first up, many would have thought he was being insensitive to the occasion, but he pressed on. "I'll tell you who he thought he was . . . He thought he was a discerning man of God who had experience that wouldn't be wasted, experience that would help others, and experience that ultimately would help me come to the place you see depicted in this picture," he said as he pointed toward the easel.

"Greg and I individually and, at different seasons, relapsed multiple times after getting sober and off the drugs. But I can tell you that although we didn't come to a saving grace in Christ and experience his mercy at the same times, when we each did, we became new creatures, just like it says in scripture. Like it says in 2 Corinthians 5:17, 'Therefore, if anyone is in Christ, he is a new creation; the old has gone, the new has come'.

"We are new creatures, and if God can be merciful and have grace to a guy like me, he can for anybody."

He looked around the room and continued, "If you have friends that are not saved by grace through Jesus Christ, our Lord, I implore you to continue to pray for them, spend time with them, and don't give up on them. If they respond *no* a hundred times, go another hundred times until they get the importance of the message. Keep inviting them to things like that men's retreat I talked about earlier until they go. Don't give up if they don't get it the first time around. One attribute I so appreciated and admired about Greg was his persistence. He absolutely was relentless and wouldn't give up on a lost soul, especially this one. I'm sure glad he didn't."

"Grace is defined as favor or as a gift freely given by God. Mercy is defined as compassion shown toward offenders by a person charged with administering justice. Don't let those you love not experience God's grace and mercy because you believe they are too hardened to receive it. Love them into it. It can be done, trust me. That's what Greg did for this brother. You do it for those you love. Don't give up. It's the most important decision every human being needs to make. It's a matter of life and death in the hereafter. Thank you"

At this, JD concluded and began his walk back to his seat, greeted by light applause from the audience, which crescendoed to a point that indicated people not only got his message today, but realized they were committing to his challenge with each clap of their hands. I, on the other hand, realized I was one of those brothers he spoke of, one to not give up on. How I didn't want to admit that but knew in my heart that it was true. I was one of those who'd wandered off, due in large part to my anger at Christ. I pondered how many times and how many ways Dad had tried to get me to see the truth of Christ and make sure I had my eternal destiny locked up. Why was I so stubborn?

I continued to have doubts about God's love for me. I stacked up all the evidences of God in my life, and even though I believed in God, I really didn't see Him as someone who really loved or even cared about me as an individual. Why should I believe He cared about me, right? After all, He'd allowed me and my sister to be hearing impaired from birth. He allowed my dad to become an alcoholic/addict who wasn't there for me more than half of my life. He caused my mom to suffer through depression for a number of years. He let Mom and Dad go through years of strife in our home, which almost ended in divorce just a little over a year ago. He hadn't provided a job for me for what now totaled six months after graduation. To add insult to injury, He now was letting me (and my sister) lose our sight slowly but surely with retinitis pigmentosa, just one more stupid congenital disease that I'd have to endure. And the latest confirmation that God didn't care about me: allowing my best friend in life, my dad, to die of a brain tumor.

Even with all these signs of an unloving and uncaring God, I was sensing from today that God's love for me shouldn't be determined by circumstances in life. It still was confusing as thoughts swirled through my head, but I knew that I loved my dad with all my heart, even in spite of all the pain he'd caused our family. Maybe I should consider a similar love of God. Those two still seemed to not have parallel paths for me, so I dismissed the thought. I obviously needed to get out of my own head, so I refocused and forged forward with the service at hand.

# CHAPTER 17

I KNEW THIS EVENT was going to be harder with Dad not there, but for some reason, it was affecting me more than I would want to admit. It was as if God himself was speaking to me through these people, but God couldn't be speaking to me and surely not through other people. That didn't even make sense, and I shook the idea as I walked up to the podium to present our fifth and final speaker of the day. I knew this one would be the most difficult person for me to present today.

"Our next and final person to speak today is someone I've known my entire life. In fact, she gave life to me and is my dad's beautiful bride, as he'd say." Before I got emotional, which I could feel was coming, I simply added, "Mom." Kyle was way ahead of me and had already placed the next painting up on the easel, after removing the last one. As Mom, who was sitting in the front row of the theater, moved gracefully toward the podium, Kyle removed the black velvet cover. I held out my hand for her once I was able to get her in my sights. I knew where she was sitting, so I reached my hand out in total darkness, hoping she was still seated in the same seat. If she hadn't been, this could have been an embarrassing situation. Fortunately, I felt her hand touch mine before I had her in view. At that moment, calmness swept over me that I'd not had all day. My mother had always had a gentle, calming spirit that seemed to follow her wherever she went, and this moment was no exception.

Once I guided her to the podium, which I was unable to see without the flashlight in hand, she began to settle in for her words to us. As I saw the screen come to life, I recognized the painted scene from a photograph I'd seen that was a mere three months old. A photograph taken during the renewal of vows ceremony in Saint Lucia. Mom had caught sight of the painting as she was nearing the podium and then she shifted her attention to the big screen in order to soak in the beach scene. She smiled with that broad beautiful smile, but I saw her lip quivering as emotion welled up inside of her. It took her a few moments to gain her composure, and I could sense that she was choking back tears, not sad tears, but tears of absolute joy.

"Well," she started, "Greg always did like to have an element of surprise in life. This painting certainly fits that trait. I knew Greg was working on a few special projects as of late. Guess I know what one of those was now."

The painting was an amazing depiction of a photograph taken by a professional photographer at Mom and Dad's renewal of vows on August 12 of this year, twenty-five years to the day from their wedding day. Dad had actually pulled off another of his many surprises in life for Mom with this ceremony. He'd coordinated the secret event with the all inclusive-resort along the northwestern shores on Saint Lucia. The resort was located in a picturesque, private bay, which had over a half mile of curved beach. The main building was level with the beach and was the central focus of the resort. It also was donned with six uniquely individual gazebos between the pools and beach, some very private and intimate and some more in the midst of the action of its guests.

The gazebos were the perfect settings for beachside weddings and renewal of vows during the day and private dinners by candlelight at night. Each one had beautiful natural surroundings and ocean views. One could order extra decorations, but the natural beauty of the trees and flowers was enough for Dad, and he didn't want to take away from its natural serenity. That was Dad's viewpoint, even before he found out it was several hundreds of dollars extra for floral decorations that could be added to a gazebo's already abundant ambiance. He tended to be frugal on some things while not sparing expense on others, a seemingly inconsistent trait of his. He determined the expense this day would be reserved for the ceremony and special touches specifically for Mom and that extra-special surprise that night during dinner at La Toc, the resort's five-star French restaurant.

Mom was brought into the loop about the renewal of vows ceremony on day 5 of their nine-day trip, the day before the actual ceremony. Her first reaction was joy, followed not far behind by panic as she didn't feel that she had an appropriate outfit for the event in a tropical venue. Not to mention another dilemma regarding what to do with her hair. Dad didn't always think these details through, but he did on this trip. He'd arranged for Mom and himself to go shopping the afternoon that he let her in on the little secret for the purchase of an acceptable dress with an island flavor. He'd already packed his attire for the ceremony, so he could focus his attention on Mom. In addition, he made an appointment (before they even boarded the plane for the flight) for Mom to have a massage and up-do immediately before the event. Although I wasn't in a serious relationship yet, I mentally filed a few of these notes away for a future time. When Mom told us about the trip and the surprise renewal when they got back, I sensed the detailed planning that Dad had done was as appreciated as much or more than the actual trip.

The dress Mom found during their afternoon shopping spree in the midst of a torrential rainstorm in Castries, the capital city, was simple and yet had a flavor of the islands. It was an off-white, empire-cut, sleeveless dress of pure cotton with modest lines with a length that cut just above the ankles. The simple gown looked like something straight out of *Mamma Mia!* and, even though off the rack, looked like it had been custom-made for Mom. It fit her personality as well as everything else, simple, elegant, and understated.

The ceremony itself was planned to take place in one of the more private of gazebos on the beach, complete with bouquet and boutonniere for the couple, created with native flowers to the island. The most striking flower in their bouquet and boutonniere was the orange bird-of-paradise. A single orange bird-of-paradise with a touch of baby's breath made up the boutonniere; however, the orange flower was just one of more than a half dozen native flowers in the bouquet, most of which I did not recognize. The renewal package also included appropriate music, a judge to preside over the ceremony, hors d'oeuvres, cake, and champagne. Of course, they added nonalcoholic sparkling cider for Dad, but Mom enjoyed the champagne. Knowing Mom, she only had one glass during the actual ceremony, her typical, self-imposed limit.

The couple began their ceremony by being escorted from the wedding chapel to the gazebo by an attendant. The chapel served as an office but was used as a backup for ceremonies during inclement weather. Sunny skies graced them this day, so no inside ceremony this particular day. They strode from the chapel to a stone sidewalk about fifty yards shy of the gazebo. There was another attendant at the base of the gazebo and the dark-skinned native judge in her sixties, who'd be conducting the ceremony. The judge had her Bible tucked under her arm, and there was a photographer at the end of the walkway, already taking pictures of them by the time they stepped onto the natural stone walkway.

Dad and Mom hadn't walked down the aisle together during their original wedding ceremony twenty-five years ago, but instead Mom's dad walked her down the aisle in traditional fashion. One thing that was exactly the same was the music that was played, which was their cue to begin walking toward the gazebo from the end of the pathway. Pachelbel's Canon in D began playing, and Dad and Mom both broke out into broad smiles, not for the camera, but toward each other as they had a shared flashback to their wedding day.

Exactly twenty-five years ago, Dad, his groomsmen, and the pastor were all in a hallway just beyond doors in the front of the big Baptist church they attended at the time in St. Louis, awaiting their time to make their grand entrance, setting the stage for the wedding scene. However, when the pastor calmly asked Dad and his groomsmen what song they were supposed to walk out to, no one knew. One of the groomsmen remembered and told the group that it was that "Pocabell Cannon thing" to which Dad confidently said, "Oh yeah, Pachelbel's Canon in D. Whew, I'll know that when it plays." Wrong. He wouldn't have done well with *Name That Tune* as he had the entourage walk out on *Jesu, Joy of Man's Desiring*, long before the mothers had even been seated. He was oblivious to the blunder, still not realizing he'd messed up their entrance even after he saw the mothers being escorted down to be seated.

Mom, the calming force for most of their marriage, asked the wedding planner if the guys had made it out yet just before the doors were opened wide and she and her dad made the grandest of entrances. "Oh yeah, they've been out there for a while," she replied. Mom thought the response to be odd and didn't realize that there was more to the response than she wanted to know. After the ceremony, the truth about Dad's premature arrival came out at the reception in discussion, and Mom just stated simply, "I had a feeling you had messed up somewhere today, which lines up there with our first date when you dropped pizza in your lap and lost the movie theater tickets. I hope this isn't a foreshadowing of things to come with you."

They both recalled Dad's blunder from their wedding day, then retreated back into the current moment, the beginning of their vow renewal. Both of them wanted to soak in every moment, and their entire focus was truly on each other, which was made easier since there were no guests in their private event.

Once they made their way to the gazebo and walked carefully up the steps, they were guided by the judge to the back center of the white-stained wooden-and-lattice structure. All the while, the photographer was taking candid shots with breathtaking views of the ocean from virtually every angle. It was truly hard to mess up a photo with such beautiful surroundings. The reading of vows began once they were positioned into place by the judge. When the repeating of vows began, Dad was first. He got so choked up with emotion that he was able to only mouth the words, and the faintness of his voice through his tears caused the judge to take pause and look closely at him to make sure she wasn't losing him. Once she was assured that he was repeating the vows, even if barely audible, she continued through the vow renewals.

Dad's emotion during repeating of the vows had a stark similarity to their vows from twenty-five years earlier. Dad didn't make it through two words during their wedding ceremony before he choked up with emotion both then and now. Mom felt compelled back then to squeeze him like an accordion to get the words out of him, which was effective. This time around, though, Mom did something she hadn't done during their wedding ceremony. She stared deeply into Dad's eyes, into his soul, and began to openly weep, tears streaming down her face. When her time came to repeat after the judge, she too was barely audible for the judge to hear as she was having her own issue with emotion. The judge just kept checking each of them to make sure that lips were actually moving to form the words she was asking them to repeat before she moved to the next parts of the vows.

The server, photographer, and presiding judge had seen emotion during ceremonies before, but they could sense that there was something different this time, a sense of painful struggle and joyful triumph with the couple before them. What they couldn't know was how significant and painful the struggles had been. They wouldn't be privy to the facts that this loving, emotional couple had been separated for over five months with divorce papers served to the husband, that this couple had mourned loss they'd had with their children over their genetic hearing losses and sight impairment of their son, that there were years of alcohol and drug abuse as a coping tool that impacted the whole family, or could they have known about the recent diagnosis of the short-term terminal illness that was about to take Dad's life. Little did they know that Dad wouldn't live to see their twenty-sixth year together. What they could see was that this couple before them was in a dimension of love they rarely saw during these ceremonies and that the couple was soaking in each precious moment of the day.

Yes, the couple that renewed their vows that day on the beautiful shores of Saint Lucia had a newfound love beyond what most find in a lifetime, a love that had Christ truly as the center. One verse requested to be added to the Saint Lucia renewal of vows, which was so befitting, was Ecclesiastes 4:12, "A cord of three strands is not quickly broken." That summed up that day on the beach, long before the reading of 1 Corinthians 13 and the "You may now kiss your bride."

The painting that filled up the movie screen while the two to three foot original sat majestically on the easel in the front center of the theater was one of Dad's best pieces he'd ever completed. He had captured a moment from that special August day, the basis of which was one of the photographs he and Mom had purchased as part of a package from the resort.

I knew the picture well as it was the five-by-seven I'd selected of the two of them for the desk in my room. The scene was brilliant with color, the light tan sandy beach in the foreground and the blue green aqua color of the sea in the middle with light, breaking whitecaps coming ashore, along with a bright blue sky with scattered clouds of pure white. In the midst of the painting were Mom and Dad, walking in oblivion to the world that surrounded them, both looking downward, absorbed in each other during their stroll just inside the ocean waters that were rolling ashore.

Both were barefoot, and with Dad's dark chocolate brown slacks rolled up and Mom's hand holding a gathered section of her dress, it appeared they were safe from getting their dress clothes wet from the gentle rolling waves running ashore. Mom held a colorful bouquet of flowers, dominated by large orange birds-of-paradise, loosely in her other arm. Dad was donning an off-white, straw hat with a chocolate brown band around it and had on a light tan shirt with the sleeves rolled up to complete his ensemble. Mom's hair from her up-do was pulled up into a loose bun with small white flowers that had been picked that morning and placed across the top of her hair, serving as a natural tiara. Mom's face was mostly visible in the painting, even with her downward glance toward Dad's feet, but Dad's face was virtually blocked by the straw hat. Knowing Dad and his lack of desire to be photographed, this seemed an appropriate pose for him to choose to paint.

The only visible sign of Dad's face was a broad smile, which showed below the brim of the hat. Mom's brilliant smile completed the picture. It was apparent that this painting was of a couple that was completely absorbed in their love for each other. The love could almost be felt, emanating from the canvas.

Mom, while still glancing back and forth toward the painting or the screen filled with Dad's creation, addressed the audience once again. "As you've heard here today, Greg wanted us to talk to you not about him but about Christ and what He can mean to you, ultimately wanting to make sure that you know that you know that you know, as JD stated, that your salvation is solid, no doubts whatsoever."

She added, "Greg, in his usual OCD fashion," to which there were several chuckles from those who knew that was so much a part of his DNA, "had a specific order for all of us today." She looked around the room, imploring everyone with her eyes to grasp what she was saying. "You heard Renee talk about the legacy of Christ and God's Word, demonstrating so well how that has such a dramatic and eternal impact that you . . . you . . . can make on generations to come. You heard RT speak to us about unconditional love, the love we have for each other, and most importantly the love that our Maker has for every single one of us, a love that we truly cannot understand with our finite human minds. He spoke of a love that caused our Creator to allow His only Son to die on a cross not just for your and my sins but for the world from the beginning to the end of times."

Mom paused here, removing what we referred to as her Sarah Palin-like glasses, placing the end of one of its arms to the edge of her mouth and then in a pensive and thoughtful delivery, said "Greg used to say that he couldn't imagine just his sin from his life being placed on a person, whether part God and part man or not, on a cross. Greg would add at this point, 'Think about that . . . The enormity of just one person's sin on Christ at the cross. Now think about an entire family's sins put upon our savior, then our town, then all mankind.'" Dad would shake his head just thinking about the magnitude of this and say something like "You'd think Jesus would have just imploded on that cross." She chuckled as did many others in the audience and then continued, "That made no sense to any of us, but we always just listened to humor him. We knew what he meant, and it certainly helps us realize the magnitude of God's unbelievable love for each of us."

"So RT helped us realize that love is truly the greatest gift of all, demonstrated so dramatically by our Lord and savior."

She added, "Lindsey then painted a picture of redemption and forgiveness, a story more like 'the prodigal dad' than the prodigal son, helping us to realize that it's never too late. Helping us realize that every one of us has the opportunity to be forgiven and redeemed while still here on this earth."

"JD then gave us a great visual of God's grace and mercy. As he pointed out, none of us, not one person in this auditorium today, is worthy of God's grace and mercy. And it doesn't matter what you've done. God's grace truly is sufficient, and his mercy is immense."

She breathed deeply and then proceeded, "And I'm wrapping up today with telling you about hope. Greg and I are poster children for hope, a couple who has faced adversity on steroids and come through it with a hope that others can see without having to look very far. A couple who have two wonderful children who were afflicted with hearing as well as eyesight challenges with our son. We never called it and we will never call it a handicap as it's more of an inconvenience in this life than anything else. Regardless, for those of you with children, you know that you are most vulnerable with your kids, and you want only the best for them and nothing less . . . We have that, but we didn't always see that."

As she looked toward me with that crooked pursed-lips smile, I felt her love radiate from her heart into mine. She refocused and continued, "We lived through addiction issues, and even after it was brought from darkness into light, we dealt with multiple relapses, losing trust all the while and wondering if that trust would ever come back. Separation followed by what seemed an imminent divorce, just one more piece of our story. A career loss, threatening our security in the midst of putting our youngest through college, and with all of these, our story's far from being over."

"Adding insult to injury, finding out the head of our home had a terminal illness that would take him away from us in a very short time frame, which made us wonder about that verse about God not putting you through more than you can handle. There are times in all our lives when we believe we've passed that threshold of pain, believing we are being put through more than we can handle. There is truth in that . . . We can't handle it on our own strength and power, but we can if we truly rely on Christ."

She opened a Bible that was stored underneath the podium and said, "Let me read that right now as it was a promise that our family has read more than once over the years. 1 Corinthians 10:13 declares,

'No temptation has seized you except what is common to man. And God is faithful; he will not let you be tempted beyond what you can bear. But when you are tempted, he will also provide a way out so that you can stand up under it.' When you believe you cannot handle the pain that this life is dealing you, read this over and over, hiding this promise in your heart." She paused, adding "It doesn't promise that we won't go through difficulties, nor does it promise that He won't take you through more than you can bear, which is what most of us think it says . . . It promises that He will help us stand up to temptations during these rough times and provide us a way out. This helps me know that when I'm weak, He can be counted on to be my strength."

Mom stopped in her tracks and turned her head slowly and deliberately toward the painting and pointed at it. "I look at the loving couple you see in this painting, which I'll treasure so much for the rest of my days and you know what I see? I see hope . . . Hope for those of you that think life is ending, hope for those of you that think it cannot get any worse, and hope for those of you that believe God doesn't care about you anymore." That last comment really struck a chord with me, and it seemed as though Mom was reading my mind. I knew at that moment that I had been relying on my strength to get through life. Why was I being so hard-headed and not looking to Him to help me get through life's difficult circumstances?

She continued, "He provided us a glimmer of hope when Greg and I agreed to try counseling for the third time during the midst of separation and what appeared to be an inevitable divorce. He gave us another glimpse of hope when our children grew up to become the amazing adults they are now . . . That after getting the devastating news many years ago that they both had severe hearing loss, which now seems like such a trivial issue in the big scheme of things. We've sensed that we need to continue to hope for sight for our son, who was dealt this new challenge a year ago, when he was diagnosed with retinitis pigmentosa and Usher syndrome. Even though the diagnosis of the disease is eventual loss of his sight, a disease that has no known cure and no proven treatment, we have hope for a treatment or cure whether in this lifetime or the next, knowing that God is trustworthy and sovereign in this situation. He gave us full sight of hope in eternity with our Father in heaven when Greg . . ." Mom stopped in midsentence as she looked back toward a set of double doors in the auditorium, which caused most of us to do the same.

# CHAPTER 18

THE COMMOTION IN the back of the room began as the double doors were opening, and of all things, Dad is wheeled into the room in a wheelchair by a person that a handful of us recognized, a friend of the family from church, the nurse who requested to attend to Dad during what we believed to be his final days. We were all stunned at his presence. The last we'd seen of him, he was in a comatose state. Dr. Slaughter said that he would most likely stay comatose and simply go into a permanent sleep. There had been a very short debate on canceling today's funeral service after Dad's episode from yesterday, but Mom had told us with no uncertain terms that Dad insisted that this service go on, no matter what happened.

Dad had insisted that this day should be more about Christ anyway, and canceling this service would only draw attention back to him and not Him. We had quickly agreed that the "show" must go on, knowing Mom was right. What had been hardest thing for most of us today was not knowing if Dad would already be with his Maker before the end of the service. It was something all of us agreed we would not discuss or address during the service but rather that we'd update everybody on the last twenty-four hours and Dad's current state before we walked into that auditorium for the service. Amazingly, everyone complied with that request, no one referring to Dad's comatose state in intensive care. We'd even asked the hospital to not interrupt the service should something happen. Obviously, they hadn't complied with our last request, but somehow, no one seemed disturbed with this particular interruption.

Mom had a tremendous amount of trouble regaining her composure, and the audience broke into growing applause while he was wheeled to the front of the auditorium. The entire place gave a standing ovation to which Dad, in an obvious weakened condition, waved them down, not in a "more, more" way, but in a way that made everyone know this day really wasn't to be focused on him.

Mom walked part way up the theater aisle to him, gave him a full kiss on the lips, and walked back to the podium to finish what she'd started. "Well, nothing like being interrupted by the eight hundred-pound gorilla who decides to enter the room." Laughs of joy filtered throughout the auditorium with that comment.

"There's also nothing like being thrown for a loop twice while speaking to a group. I have no idea where I was going before I was so rudely interrupted by the most wonderful man in my life on this earth . . . So . . ."

Mom took a deep breath as emotions once again were building within her. She couldn't seem to look anywhere but at Dad now that he was in our midst, constantly glancing his way, but she kept on task. "Let me just conclude my last thought. God has given us full sight of eternity. Greg will be seeing our Father in Heaven soon, and there is not a doubt in our minds about his destination – a fulfillment of hope and a lot of prayers. We also have a hope that each one of you will be reunited with Greg someday but, most importantly, that you'll spend eternity in heaven with our heavenly Father as well."

"Greg asked that we focus on Christ today, and I believe that is exactly what was done here today. Although I hate that he missed . . ." She caught herself again, looking right at Dad to address him. "Although I hate that you missed a large portion of today, Greg, I'm grateful that you are able to join us even if just for a short while as we conclude. I've learned from you, Greg, to focus on what we have and not what we've lost. That will be a mantra for me the remainder of my days, and I thank you for that as well as for that wonderful gift on that easel," she said as she pointed toward the center of the room. "A treasure of love and hope for the remainder of my days to gaze upon." Instinctively, she crossed her arms over her chest in what our family all knew was sign language for love. Although we never fully learned sign language, we knew some words just from watching interpreters at church over the years who helped those who had little to no hearing be able to "hear" the worship and message.

As she refocused her energies toward all of us, she said, "And for all the rest of you, wonderful family and friends, we thank you for being here today and pray that each and every one of you have searched your own souls here today, reflecting on your eternal destiny, and for indulging us in such a nontraditional service. We love you and so does our Lord Jesus Christ."

I knew we were wrapping up the day's events with one last item, and although a full hour and forty-five minutes had passed, I was not ready for this service to end. There was an unexplainable tug on me that I couldn't fully put my finger on or explain, something that gave me comfort and peace but that also was challenging me. As Kyle pulled the last painting off the easel, setting it gently against a far wall, the big screen came to life on cue. It was filled once again with Dad's image, sitting in another of his favorite spots, in a golf cart near a green, surrounded by water. I recognized the setting as it was a hole that we'd played a couple of years ago when Dad took me for a round of golf. The green reminded me of the seventeenth hole at Sawgrass in Florida, but it was just a public course in Algonquin, one that Dad typically played once or twice a month during golf season. Being a rather frugal individual, he would never consider a club membership for the limited amount of times a year he played. Instead, he'd spend $50 – 75 a round with cart, playing two to three times a month.

He looked into the camera, dressed as if he was ready to play a round, in a black collared shirt and tan pleated shorts, with short golf socks, black-and-white oxford golf shoes and black glove on his left hand. The one constant companion when outdoors was with him too, one of about a hundred baseball caps, this one tan to coordinate with his outfit, of course. Even though he looked like he walked off the pages of a golf magazine, I knew that most likely, none of his outfit was designer clothing. He was not into the designer scene as he thought it bad stewardship, but if he got a 70 percent discount off retail, he might just buy the nicer stuff.

Dad looked into the camera and began his wrap up. "Well, I really appreciate you being at the funeral service today. You most likely will never attend another one quite like this and may be thinking, 'And am I ever glad for that.'"

He smiled broadly and continued, "Whether I am there today or not really isn't important. What is, though, is what you put into your heart." He lightly pounded his heart with his right balled-up hand. "And take with you from here and into eternity."

He grabbed the handle on the roof of the white golf cart, lifted himself easily out and stood, walking slowly as the camera followed his steps. The clip had the professionalism of a commercial or at least an infomercial, but it wasn't cheesy but rather comforting. "I pray that this is the catalyst for life changes for some of you. Don't worry, I won't name you," to which nervous laughter was heard from a number of folks in the theater. "Thanks again for being here, and if I'm not there, my heartfelt desire is to see you again, in a place we can call home forever, where our heavenly Father resides and where we can live truly happy, joyous, and free. No more heartache, no more disease, no more struggles, a place that you absolutely want to be. As it states in Revelations 21:4, 'He will wipe every tear from their eyes. There will be no more death or mourning or crying or pain, for the old order of things has passed away.'" As he continued to walk slowly around the lake surrounding the hole, he added, "I do have one more special surprise for the only person in my immediate family who didn't get one of the paintings."

Those near me were looking at me, and I just smiled, looking around for a painting that might be coming my way. Instead, as I glanced at my mother, she was getting out of her seat and approaching me with a large envelope in tow, which definitely didn't give me a clue, but just added to my confusion. Dad continued, "Jared, your mother is probably walking toward you about now." As he hesitated, I said aloud, "Well, you got that right, Dad." Those around me that could hear my comment chuckled. "This was my last major project, and you were a major part of it without even realizing it."

By now, I'm really baffled and have no clue what he's talking about. But I'm very intrigued to learn more. Dad, a man always full of surprises.

"What your mother is presenting to you about now," he continued as mom delivered a large package into my hands without a word, "is a manuscript of a book I've written over the last five months, a book that will appear to have been written by you, when you read it."

I'm just looking over at Dad now instead of the screen, totally perplexed as seen by the almost visible question mark in the expression on my face.

"This book is the story of a man whose last desire after finding out about a terminal illness is to have a funeral service with his friends and relatives at one of his favorite venues – a movie theater."

I grin but still not following his comments.

Dad adds, "Sound a little familiar?"

"The focus of the service in the book is Christ and his love, peace, hope, grace, and mercy, as well as the legacy that we should hope to leave for generations to come, one that leads them to either where I am or where I'm heading – my Father's house, where streets are of pure gold."

Now, I'm almost freaking out as it's as if the tape that I'm viewing has happened after today's events. I'm thinking, *How in the world would you be able to write a book that speaks to exactly what took place here today?*

"Jared, the book is written as if you're the author of the story, but the twist is that in reality, it's your dad that is writing from your vantage point, from your eyes . . . Those beautiful big brown puppy-dog eyes of yours."

At this, those big brown puppy-dog eyes begin to tear up, clouding my vision. "But there's another twist, Budster . . . The final chapter hasn't been written, and I'm leaving this book in your competent hands to complete."

Now, tears are streaming down my cheeks as I realized the impact of what Dad is telling me and encouraging me to do. "Bud, I leave this gift with you to complete as you see fit. I love you and everyone who is here today." At this, I'm an absolute wreck, and the last several years of my life begin to flash quickly in my mind . . . My disappointments, my anger with God for allowing my sister and I to be severely hearing impaired, my anger with my dad for causing us to live with an addict for most of my life, my anger with both parents for the fear and desperation I felt during their separation and near divorce, my rage over the recent diagnosis that seems to be leading me into a lifetime of darkness, and the hopelessness I was feeling with the imminent loss of my dad.

I felt so humbled at this point, realizing how self-centered I'd been, how I'd not relied on Christ's strength, and how I'd lost hope, trusting in myself as opposed to my Creator. There was no doubt in my mind that a transformation was occurring within me at this very moment. Circumstances had dictated my contentment and joy for too long, and I was worn out from trying to do life on my own. I could sense this was all about to change. The road map was not clear for how this change would take place, but there was no doubt in my mind that the future would be brighter. All I could see before today was darkness in my future, literally and figuratively; now, I could see a brighter future – a life full of life and peace.

Dad is wrapping up his final comment as tears are filtering throughout the auditorium, and I'm feeling an unbelievable weight, but at the same time, I'm feeling that weight lifting off me as well. Dad continued, "Thanks to each of you, and Bud," as I now peered up into the eyes of the man on the screen, "enjoy writing that last chapter. I promise you, it will be a blast."